"You're the most annoying girl I've ever come across."

Dominic's tone was grim. "Not content with damaging my car and causing me the maximum amount of embarrassment in London, you then turn up here, in Norfolk, marching into the house without an invitation."

"I was invited!"

"... And within only a few hours, you're championing my brother's mad ideas, causing friction at the dinner table, asking extremely impertinent questions and generally creating mayhem."

"Me...? Creating mayhem?" She blinked at him in astonishment.

"Oh, yes. I can think of other words that would do as well," he continued, "words like chaos, commotion, havoc and trouble. But *mayhem* is definitely the word that comes to mind whenever I think about you, Kate!"

MARY LYONS is happily married to an Essex farmer, has two children and lives in an old Victorian rectory. Life is peaceful—unlike her earlier years when she worked as a radio announcer, reviewed books and even ran for parliament in a London dockland area. She still loves a little excitement and combines romance with action and suspense in her books whenever possible.

Books by Mary Lyons

MARY LYONS

Dark and Dangerous

Harlequin Books

TORONTO • NEW YORK • LONDON
AMSTERDAM • PARIS • SYDNEY • HAMBURG
STOCKHOLM • ATHENS • TOKYO • MILAN
MADRID • WARSAW • BUDAPEST • AUCKLAND

Harlequin Presents first edition October 1992
ISBN 0-373-11499-0

Original hardcover edition published in 1991
by Mills & Boon Limited

DARK AND DANGEROUS

PROLOGUE

'How does the defendant plead? Guilty or not guilty?'

A bright shaft of sunlight, streaming in through the high windows of the London courtroom, shone down upon the tall figure of a girl standing in the dock. Brushing a slim, nervous hand through her cloud of tawny-gold hair, she hesitated for a moment.

'Have I *really* got to choose one or the other?' she asked, gazing anxiously up at the elderly stipendiary magistrate seated on his raised dais. 'How about, "Yes, I'm sort of guilty—but it was all a dreadful mistake"?'

'That won't do, I'm afraid,' he told her kindly but firmly.

'But I've promised to tell the truth, the whole truth and nothing but the truth. So why can't I just explain what happened?'

The magistrate sighed, adjusting his glasses as he peered down at the documents in front of him. 'I believe you are a visitor to this country, Miss Macaulay?'

'Yes, sir. I'm over here from Canada—just staying for a while in England, before going on a tour of Europe.'

'And I understand that you are intending to represent yourself in this court?'

'Sure—why not? I've heard all about British justice, and I guess you'll see that I have a fair trial. You will—won't you?' she added, giving the elderly man a warm pleading smile.

'Oh, yes...er...indeed...' he muttered, clearing his throat nervously. 'However, Miss Macaulay, before we can start hearing the evidence, you must tell the court whether you wish to plead guilty or not guilty.'

'Well, I really can't decide what to do. It's all so difficult, you see. On the one hand...'

The girl paused, a deep flush spreading across her cheeks as a tall man, dressed in a dark formal suit, strode purposefully into the courtroom. Carrying a briefcase in one hand, the cords of a red bag slung over his shoulder, he gave a slight nod to the magistrate before lowering himself down on one of the front benches.

'I'm sorry to be late, Alan,' he muttered to the man sitting beside him. 'How's it going?'

'It isn't!' his solicitor grinned. 'The lady is still trying to make up her mind whether or not she's guilty.'

'Of course she's guilty!' Dominic Smith-Farrell grated in a low, angry voice as he turned his stormy eyes on the girl in the dock. 'I caught her red-handed, didn't I?'

'Well, I must admit I wouldn't mind getting my "red hands" on that particular girl,' his old friend murmured, gazing at Miss Macaulay's generously curved figure with frank appreciation.

'Humph!' Dominic grunted dismissively. He had never been attracted to the very tall, Junoesque type of woman—and goodness knows, that girl must be at least six feet tall in her stockinged feet. With her flowing mane of sun-streaked, amber-coloured hair brushed back from her wide brow, over large blue eyes which bore an almost feline expression, she bore, he had thought, on their first encounter, an uncanny resemblance to a fierce tigress. However, it was now a tigress with sheathed claws, he noted, his gaze narrowing as he saw the girl give the magistrate another warm, friendly smile.

His solicitor shrugged. 'In any case, guilty or not, it looks as if Miss Macaulay is managing to wind old Parkinson around her little finger.'

'Senile old fool! He should have retired from the bench years ago,' Dominic muttered grimly, casting a scathing glance up at the elderly magistrate before turning his dark head to look around the courtroom. 'Am I going to be required to give evidence?'

'I don't think so. However, from the way this case is going, I wouldn't like to bet on it.'

'That's all I need—especially as I've only got half an hour before I'm due in the High Court.' Dominic's foot tapped impatiently, his lips tightening into a hard line as he stared at the tall girl. 'As far as I'm concerned, she deserves to be hanged, drawn and quartered!' he added grimly.

'...Let me see if I can help you, Miss Macaulay,' the magistrate was saying, clearly bending over backwards to assist the girl in the dock. 'Did you go to Wilton Street on the day in question?'

'Yes, sir, I did.'

'And while there, did you see a red sports car parked beside the road, a few yards away from a large vehicle carrying fresh cement?'

'Yes, sir. That's what gave me the idea, you see?' The girl brushed nervous, trembling fingers through her long hair. 'I was so furiously cross and angry with the rotten, two-timing rat—— Er...um...I mean...er...the man I'd been involved with...' she amended quickly as the magistrate frowned down at her. 'It wasn't just the fact that he'd proved to be so unfaithful which upset me so much,' she explained. 'I'd also just found out that he'd stolen some of my money.'

'If you could just keep to the point, Miss Macaulay...?'

'Well, I knew my boyfriend had an apartment in Wilton Street, and that he drove around in an open red sports car,' the girl muttered, clearly embarrassed at having to relate in open court the story of her disastrous romance. 'I guess I was a fool—a complete idiot, right?' she continued with flushed cheeks. 'Because I just naturally assumed the car belonged to him. I'd only been in it one or two times—and I honestly don't know one make of English automobile from another. As far as I could see, the car in Wilton Street was just the same old wreck that my boyfriend had been driving around town.' She gave a helpless shrug.

'What does she mean—an *old wreck*? That car was my pride and joy!' Dominic hissed, staring malevolently at the girl in the dock.

'...And so when I saw that cement truck—well, I guess I must have had some sort of brainstorm.' The girl shook her head in distress. 'Because when I looked in the cab and saw that the driver had gone off, leaving the key in the ignition, it didn't take me five seconds to back up the truck, pull a lever—and tip a whole load of cement into the open sports car.'

The magistrate frowned as a ripple of laughter ran around the courtroom. 'But, as I understand it, Miss Macaulay, the vehicle in question was *not* owned by...er...the person against whom you had such a strong grudge. That, in fact, it belonged to a complete stranger—the distinguished lawyer, Mr Dominic Smith-Farrell, QC.'

'Yes...that's what's so awful, you see. I did make the most dreadful mistake. And I truly am *very* sorry that I picked the wrong car.' The girl cast a nervous sideways glance at Dominic's tall figure sitting on a bench across the courtroom.

'What absolute rubbish! She wasn't at all sorry!' Dominic whispered savagely, grinding his teeth at the recollection of the strange girl's wild, hysterical laughter as his beloved car had disappeared beneath an avalanche of cement.

'I know that what I did was very wrong. But maybe if Mr Smith-Farrell hadn't been so furious, spending so much time screaming blue murder, before dragging me off to the police station...?' The girl gave a heavy sigh. 'Well, maybe the quick-drying cement wouldn't have had time to harden. Unfortunately, by the time someone did come along to dig out the car, I'm afraid it was far too late.'

'It certainly was!' Dominic agreed grimly under his breath.

The magistrate cleared his throat. 'Since it appears, Miss Macaulay, that you're prepared to admit...'

'Oh, sure,' the girl interrupted, vigorously nodding her head. 'I'm perfectly willing to admit that I committed—what do you call it?—"malicious damage"? And, although it's taken a few days to arrange the transfer of money from Canada, I've now paid the insurance company for the loss of the car. However, I do want to assure the court that it was all a dreadful mistake; that I had no intention of destroying Mr Smith-Farrell's car; and...well, I guess I'd like to tell him again just how very sorry I am,' she added, wincing as she cast another quick, nervous glance at the hard stony expression on Dominic's face.

The magistrate peered down over his glasses at the black-gowned clerk of the court. 'The sum involved does not appear to be excessively large. Do we have any further information on this matter?'

'Yes, sir.' The clerk stood up. 'I understand that the insurance company has been paid in full.'

'Well, in that case...'

'All right, Alan, that's it—I'm off!' Dominic muttered angrily, not waiting to hear any more as he rose quickly to his feet. 'Not only has this morning been a complete waste of time, but I'm also quite certain that horrendous girl—who's succeeded in making me look such a fool—is going to get off scot free. As far as I'm concerned, *the law is an ass*!' he added bitterly, his anger fuelled by the fact that his solicitor had obviously found the proceedings as amusing as the rest of the court.

Quickly rising and hurrying after his client as he strode purposefully from the courtroom, the solicitor grinned up at his old friend, who had recently been described as 'a high flier...one of the most successful lawyers in the country'.

'You haven't done too badly,' he pointed out. 'At least your insurance company has been paid, and there's nothing to stop you buying another "old wreck". Incidentally, I thought Miss Macaulay's description of your antique roadster was absolutely spot on!'

'Humph!' Dominic snorted grimly as he turned to leave the courtroom. 'Let me tell you, Alan, that my only consolation in this whole miserable affair is to know that the awful Miss Macaulay will soon be leaving Britain—hopefully never, *ever* to return!'

CHAPTER ONE

JUST as she was beginning to wonder whether she should have turned left instead of right at the last road junction, Kate breathed a sigh of relief as she saw the signpost: 'Thornton Magna—2 miles'.

Her aunt Laura had been extraordinarily vague and absent-minded on the telephone last week, when Kate had rung to confirm her long-standing invitation. But maybe her aunt wasn't as dim as she had sounded? Her directions on how to find Thornton Priory—set deep in the Norfolk Fenland, and surrounded by a network of confusing, narrow country roads—were proving to be surprisingly accurate.

Kate knew she ought to have been to visit her English relatives long before now. And of course, she would have done so—if it hadn't been for her disastrous encounter with Dominic Smith-Farrell...and his car.

It wasn't just that really *dreadful* mistake, which had led to her pouring cement all over his vehicle, or the humiliating experience of being arrested and appearing in court, which had caused her so much anxiety. It was when she had first heard the surname of the red sports car's owner that Kate had realised she might also be in a very deeply embarrassing situation.

She didn't know very much about her English relatives, other than the fact that her father's only and very much younger sister, Laura Macaulay, had married a Colonel Hector Smith-Farrell.

What had made her feel so sick at the time of the court case—and which had been constantly in her mind throughout her subsequent three-month tour of Europe—had been the question of just how many Smith-Farrells there were in England. It didn't strike her as a very common surname. But the British were known for possessing the most outlandish names—and for all she knew there could be thousands of people called Cholmondeley, Montmorency—or, indeed, Smith-Farrell.

Not for the first time, Kate had found herself wishing she had paid more attention to her father's stories and anecdotes. Especially those about the family he'd left behind in England, so many years ago. All she had been able to recall was that the colonel had been a widower, with a young son, when he had married her aunt Laura, and that they'd had one—or was it two?—children before the colonel had died some time ago, a year or two before her own father's death.

However, after that traumatic encounter with Dominic Smith-Farrell, and her realisation that he might possibly turn out to be some sort of relative by marriage, she had put off contacting the family until after her tour of Europe. It was only the faithful promise made to her father on his deathbed which had at last forced her to get in touch with her relatives on her return to London. And on doing so, she had found all her worst fears instantly confirmed.

'How lovely to hear from you ... dear little Katherine!' her aunt Laura had breathed huskily down the phone, her voice sounding as if she was suffering from a bad case of asthma. 'You were only four years old when we last met...such a *sweet* little thing! I was so upset to hear about your father's death...poor Tom, he was always the black sheep of the family, you know.'

'Yes, well—it's been three years since Dad died, and I'm afraid I've grown considerably larger since you last saw me,' Kate had said with a smile, before mentioning her proposed visit. She could see no point in a long, involved telephone conversation about either her present height and size, or the chequered career of her father—that charming wastrel, Thomas Macaulay.

'You must come and see us...stay as long as you like,' her aunt continued in a breathless whisper. 'How lucky that all the family are at home...I know the children will be so pleased to see you. Your visit...just the thing to cheer them up. *He's* being so difficult, you see...'

Kate had frowned, feeling confused and bewildered by the older woman's extraordinary, Alice-in-Wonderland type of conversation. How many children did Aunt Laura have? Why did they need cheering up? And whoever was the mysterious 'he', who was apparently being 'so difficult'? Surely Aunt Laura's husband, Uncle Hector, had been dead for some time?

'I'm sorry,' Kate cut ruthlessly across her aunt's breathless mumbling. 'I'm afraid I don't quite understand the problem. In fact,' she added with a slight apologetic laugh, 'I don't even know how many cousins I've got.'

'Oh dear, I'm so sorry... it's been such a long time, hasn't it? Your cousins... Martin and Alice... such lovely children, but maybe just a little *too* high-spirited? Such a clever idea... re-enacting historical events... but Helen doesn't approve and so Dominic is bound to agree with her, isn't he?'

'*Dominic?*' Kate gasped, closing her eyes with horror for a moment as she realised her usual good luck had just deserted her.

'Oh, yes... it's so easy to forget that you don't know any of us, isn't it? Dear Dominic—my stepson, you know... so very clever... such a great success at the Bar. But so... very... er... difficult at times, if you know what I mean...?'

I most certainly do! Kate thought grimly, remembering her first encounter with the dreadful man.

As her aunt continued her odd, disjointed conversation, Kate tried to pull herself together. Unfortunately, her mind seemed to be a complete blank as she frantically tried to think of a really good, valid excuse for not visiting Thornton Priory.

'... What a pity Dominic is going to be away for the next few weeks... a case in Hong Kong, I believe. How sad that you won't be able to meet him.'

On hearing the good news, Kate had immediately sagged with overwhelming relief. 'Oh, dear, I *am* sorry,' she had said insincerely, a wide grin spreading over her face as she took down her aunt's instructions on how to reach Thornton Priory.

And now, as she turned off the main road and passed through the ornate cast-iron gates set in a high brick wall which marked the boundary to the estate, Kate was still thanking her lucky stars that she had managed to avoid any further confrontation with Dominic Smith-Farrell.

Not that she was really too worried about facing the awful man, she assured herself quickly. It was just . . . well, there was no doubt that it had been a *very* acrimonious encounter. And while she could clearly understand Dominic's wrath and anger at the total destruction of his car, she was certain there was no need for him to have been quite so unnecessarily cruel and scathing—not to say downright rude!—about Kate's attempt to punish her unfaithful boyfriend.

After the sale of her family house and farm in Ontario—a measure her trustees had decided was necessary, in order to settle her father's debts—Kate hadn't really known what she wanted to do with her life. Because of her father's long terminal illness, she had worked on the family farm ever since leaving school. Having to make all the major decisions to do with crops and livestock had been a hard if at times rewarding life. Unfortunately, the net result was that she had now reached the age of twenty-four, only to find herself thoroughly ill-equipped to earn her living in any profession other than farming. However, she did have a very small private income, arising from the money which was left after all her father's debts had been paid, and so she'd decided to go on a tour of Europe before returning to Canada and settling down to train for some sort of career.

Kate's first port of call had been on her old school friend Jayne Bailey, with whom she had always kept in touch. Jayne, who had left Canada for Britain some years ago, was now working for a well-known publishing company in London. They'd both had a lot of fun together but, unfortunately, it was a party given by Jayne for her old friend which had brought that smoothie, Charles Yorke, into Kate's life.

What a rat-fink the man had turned out to be! Even now, three months after the event, Kate found it difficult to understand how she could have been so blind. She'd had lots of casual boyfriends in Canada—although she hadn't taken any of them very seriously, mostly because she was so busy working on her father's farm. But how on earth could she have allowed herself to become so mesmerised by the rotten man? And in such a short space of time too?

Kate found herself almost writhing with embarrassment as she looked back on her inane, foolish behaviour. Being wined and dined, and treated as though she was made of fragile porcelain, had certainly gone to her stupid head. But never again! she promised herself grimly, only too thankful that Jayne's words of caution had finally broken through the thick mist of adoration with which she had regarded Charles.

'I hardly know the guy,' Jayne had pointed out hesitantly. 'But I've heard rumours that he's heavily involved with a very rich French girl, and spends a lot of time flying back and forth to Paris. Which may account for the fact that he's never available at weekends. And if he can afford the cost of the flights, how come you, Kate, always seem to pick up the tab whenever you go out with the guy?'

Once she had been persuaded to take a good, hard look at both Charles and her relationship with him, Kate had quickly begun to realise just what a fool she'd been. And when, on that fateful day, she had confronted him with Jayne's suspicions, Charles hadn't even bothered to deny them.

'I'm looking for a rich wife, darling, and I'm afraid you simply won't do,' he had informed her with one of his charming smiles. When she had demanded the return of the money which she had temporarily loaned to him for some business deal, he had merely laughed in her face. 'You've got nothing in writing, darling, have you? So I'm afraid you're going to have to whistle for it!'

The humiliation had been too much to bear. She hadn't just been two-timed by the rat—he'd stolen her money as well! And so, almost out of her mind with rage, fury and a deep sense of grievance, Kate had slammed the door of his apartment behind her, before racing down the stairs and out into the street. As she had stood on the sidewalk, seething with anger, her eye had been caught by the sight of a large yellow cement truck parked further down the street, a few yards away from Charles's battered red sports car.

Of course, her actions during the next five minutes had been totally stupid and thoroughly illegal. But at the time it had seemed as though she was completely in the grip and power of some evil force. It wasn't until Kate found herself shaking with wild, hysterical laughter as she watched the sports car disappearing from sight beneath a torrent of dense grey cement that she had heard someone bellowing with rage as he ran down the street towards her.

'What's going on? What have you done to my car?'

Kate turned, frowning in bewilderment as she stared at the tall Englishman.

At first she wondered if she was hallucinating, because the stranger appeared to be wearing the most extraordinary, outlandish clothes. Apart from the thick mass of white lace ruffles at his throat and cuffs, he was dressed entirely in black. And 'dressed' seemed to be the appropriate word! Her eyes widened in amazement as she gazed at the figure-hugging tail-coat and knee-breeches, the black stockings covering the man's long, slim legs, and the old-fashioned black patent-leather shoes, decorated with large silver buckles.

She closed her eyes for a moment, trying to pull herself together. But when she took another hard look at the man, Kate found she hadn't been mistaken. Yes, he really *was* wearing eighteenth-century clothes! Goodness knows, she'd expected to come across some strange sights on her tour of Europe, but nothing *quite* as extraordinary as this.

Kate was jerked out of her bemused state as she became sharply aware not only of the tall, strangely dressed man's overwhelming rage and fury, but of the fact that a considerable crowd of people seemed to be gathering about them.

'I demand to know what's going on!' the man in black thundered angrily.

'You ain't the only one, mate!' a short, burly man added, pushing his way through the crowd of spectators to survey the heap of thick wet cement. 'I want to know who's been playing around with my lorry! Someone's going to have to pay for this, you know,' he added belligerently.

'Pay for this? I should damn well think they are!' the man in black retorted furiously. 'I'll have you know that my car is buried beneath that heap of cement!'

'Hang on a minute, mate,' the truck-driver interjected quickly. 'I left my vehicle up the road,' he gestured towards a house surrounded by scaffolding. 'There's no way I'm responsible for this mess.'

'Well, if *you* didn't do it, who in the hell *did*?' the tall man demanded with cold fury.

Slowly, with one accord, the two men turned to look at the girl standing beside them.

Kate gulped, a deep crimson flush spreading over her cheeks as she slowly began to realise the full, disastrous extent of her brainstorm.

The burly truck-driver took a threatening step forward. 'Have you been messing around with my lorry?' he demanded truculently, before turning to the tall stranger. 'She looks downright guilty to me, mate!'

'Yes, she does, doesn't she?' the man in black agreed in a rasping, angry voice. His icy-cold, startlingly clear blue eyes flicked contemptuously over the girl's pale face and trembling figure.

'For heaven's sake! This is nothing to do with you,' she hissed in a low voice. 'So please just go away, and let me deal with the truck-driver. OK?'

'*What . . . ?*'

'Yes, I'm afraid I did move your truck,' she told the short, burly man, trying to ignore the strangled sounds of rage coming from the tall, weirdly dressed

man standing behind her. 'I really am *very* sorry
for what I've done,' she added penitently. 'And I
will, of course, be happy to pay for that load of
cement—and for any other inconvenience I may
have caused you.'

'Yer—well, it ain't that simple, miss,' the truck-
driver told her.

'No, it certainly isn't!' the tall man in black
agreed savagely. 'What about my car?'

'Your car...? Don't be ridiculous!' snapped Kate,
fervently wishing herself a million miles away from
the street in this strange, alien city of London. Her
visit to Britain had clearly been doomed from the
start, and in the whole of her life she couldn't ever
remember feeling quite so miserable or lonely.

'I tell you it *is* my car!' the man in black was
practically dancing with rage.

'Oh, for crying out loud...!' Kate groaned,
feeling certain she was going to burst into angry,
frustrated tears at any minute. 'This is definitely
my boyfriend's car... well, my *ex*-boyfriend's car,
I guess I should say,' she added quickly as she
became aware that the altercation was attracting an
ever-increasing number of passers-by, all busy
listening to the truck-driver as he gave them a blow-
by-blow account of the incident.

Angry and confused as she was, Kate realised that
she was going to have to sort this matter out as
quickly as possible. 'Why don't you go away, and
stop interfering,' she hissed at the tall dark stranger.
'This business has absolutely nothing to do with
you!'

The strange man ground his teeth angrily
together. 'You stupid girl!' he growled, taking a

menacing step towards her. 'I parked my car here just over one hour ago. It clearly isn't anywhere else in this street,' he gestured up and down the road. 'So it must be obvious, even to someone of limited mentality such as yourself, that it is now buried beneath that mound of cement.'

Kate gave an angry snort of disbelief, refusing to allow herself to be intimidated by this crazy man. He was obviously a total weirdo. In fact, dressed in such sinister-looking clothes, and with his black hair liberally streaked with silver, she thought he bore more than a passing resemblance to Count Dracula.

'I tell you it *is* my vehicle,' he roared, visibly trembling with rage. 'And what's more, I can prove it!' he added, turning to the crowd of people surrounding them. 'If someone would just clear away the cement from the back of the car, they should be able to read my licence plate,' he explained, before quickly reciting a string of letters and numbers.

A few minutes later the truck-driver waved his grey, cement-covered hands in the air. 'It looks like you're right, mate. This does seem to be your car. So what are we all going to do now?' He gestured at the heap of grey concrete. 'I reckon this is a job for the police to sort out, don't you?'

'You're quite right,' the man in black agreed, reaching inside his tail coat for his wallet and extracting a card. 'I'll contact the local police station, and in the meantime here's my name and address. Maybe you'd tell your employers to get in touch with me regarding compensation for the loss of the cement.'

The truck-driver took the card and gave a nod of satisfaction. 'Right, mate. But what are you going to do about the girl?' He nodded towards Kate.

'There's no need for you to worry about *her*,' the man in black told him with grim satisfaction, taking hold of Kate's arm in a fierce grip. 'By the time I've finished with this young lady, she's going to wish she'd never been born!'

Kate, who had been standing dazed and bewildered as the dreadful truth slowly began to dawn on her, suddenly found herself being swept off her feet, stumbling after the man in black as he forced his way through the crowd, towing her ruthlessly behind him.

'Let me go! *Help! Police . . . !*' she cried, unable to combat the man's superior strength as he dragged her up the steps and through the open door of a large house.

'Don't worry! The very first thing I'm going to do is to call the police,' the strange man hissed through gritted teeth. Pulling her wriggling, protesting figure down a wide hall, he forcibly led her into a book-lined room, before ordering her to sit down on a wide leather couch.

'It's all right, Mrs Lewis,' he told the grey-haired woman hovering in the doorway with a shocked expression on her face. 'Just close the front door, please, and tell Horace I want to see him as soon as possible,' he added, waiting until the woman had left the room, before slowly turning to face Kate.

'Right, I want you to tell me *exactly* what is going on,' he drawled with cold menace.

'Who's that woman...?' Kate muttered, still feeling dazed as she stared up at the man regarding her with such fierce dislike.

He gave an exasperated sigh. 'Mrs Lewis is my housekeeper—but I hardly think the domestic arrangements in my house are any business of yours. Now,' he added, brushing an angry hand through his hair, 'I want your name, your address, and a brief explanation of why you poured cement all over my car.'

Kate gazed up into his icy-cold blue eyes, feeling quite sick as she at last realised that she was in desperate trouble. What could she say? What on earth had possessed her to even think of doing such a dreadful thing? Even if it *had* been Charles Yorke's car under that heap of cement, it still didn't excuse her actions. What she had done wasn't just wrong and stupid, it was also beginning to look as if she was guilty of some sort of serious crime.

'Well?' the man in black rasped curtly, impatiently drumming his fingers on a nearby table as he waited for her reply.

'Well, the thing is...' Kate took a deep breath. 'I thought... I thought that sports car belonged to my... my ex-boyfriend, you see. We'd just had a big, final row, and...' Her voice trailed away as she realised the impossibility of explaining to this man the whole sequence of events since she'd arrived in Britain.

'Oh, that's just great!' he grated savagely as he gazed fixedly down at the girl, whose cheeks were now blushing a fiery red. 'So I'm just the innocent victim of a lovers' tiff, am I?'

Kate gave a nervous gulp. 'He wasn't exactly my lover, but yes…um…yes, I do seem to have made a really bad mistake…' she mumbled, raising trembling hands to cover her face, and desperately trying to come to terms with the disaster in which she now found herself.

'You stupid girl!' he exclaimed bitterly. 'Did it never occur to you to check up on who actually owned the car before you poured cement into it?'

Kate shook her head. 'No,' she whispered miserably, desperately wishing she could sink through the floor. 'I guess—well, I guess I must have had some sort of brainstorm. But what I still don't understand…' she added, slowly beginning to pull herself together, '…is why should a guy like you—dressed in that weirdo costume—be driving around in an old heap of a car? I'd have thought a coach and horses, or maybe a Rolls-Royce, would be more your mark.'

The tall man gave an angry bark of laughter. 'As it happens I do, in fact, own a Rolls-Royce. However, that "old heap of a car", as you call it, was the very first vehicle I'd ever owned—purchased when I was a young law student at Cambridge—and I was extremely fond of it. Not that I can expect any woman, let alone a maniac such as yourself, understand what that car meant to me,' he told her grimly.

'OK, OK, I get the picture,' she muttered, staring miserably down at the Persian carpet and wishing she'd had the sense to keep her mouth shut.

'However,' the man continued in a tight, hard voice, 'while it's obviously no business of yours, you may as well know that I'm a barrister—

specialising in international commercial law. And the reason I'm wearing what might seem to be somewhat archaic clothes is that I was appointed a Queen's Counsel at Easter. In an hour's time I'm due to appear at the House of Lords to meet, among other important people, the Lord Chancellor of England. Now that might not seem very important to you,' he added scornfully, 'especially since you're obviously an American citizen, but . . .'

'Oh, no, I'm not!' Kate sat up straight on the couch. 'I'm a Canadian,' she declared proudly.

'What's the difference?' He waved an irritable hand as he strode up and down the room.

'There's a whole world of difference! We're two very different nations,' she protested.

The man in black gave a shrug of his broad shoulders. 'I'm simply not interested in your nationality,' he drawled coldly, moving over the thick carpet towards a desk at the far end of the room. 'I'm just going to telephone the police. So kindly stay right where you are—and don't you dare move an inch!' he warned her grimly.

Kate, who had had no intention of trying to escape, glared across the room at him with loathing. She'd never had the misfortune to meet such a thoroughly nasty, supercilious, male chauvinist pig. And if he thought she was impressed by all that 'Lord Chancellor' business, he was very much mistaken!

Yes, of course it was totally wrong of her to have dumped that load of cement on his car. But there was no need for him to be *so* horrid, was there? Especially since it was now crystal clear to both of them that she had simply made a very unfortunate mistake. And it was one for which Kate was quite prepared to make full restitution. She didn't have a lot of money at her disposal, but replacing that heap of old metal wasn't going to be too expensive, surely? So it looked as though her biggest problem at the moment was the involvement of the police in the matter. Could she be sent to gaol for destroying this man's car?

However, leaving aside that immediate problem, what she really couldn't stand was the man himself. Kate's normally warm, generous lips tightened as she gazed at the tall figure at the far end of the room. She couldn't hear what he was saying on the phone—but she could guarantee that the guy was going to try to make as much trouble for her as she possibly could. As far as she could see, he didn't appear to have even one drop of warm blood in those icy-cold veins of his.

Maybe, if she wasn't so darned angry with him, Kate might have been prepared to admit that the man in black was a very attractive, good-looking sort of guy. Moreover, it wasn't often that she was lucky enough to meet someone as tall, if not taller than herself—standing five feet eleven and a half inches in one's stockinged feet certainly wasn't all it was cracked up to be!

However, such thoughts were clearly a waste of time as far as this particular man was concerned. It was difficult to guess his correct age—possibly in his late thirties?—because he clearly possessed the type of dark hair which could turn prematurely white at an early age. The effect of the silvery-black, thick crop of hair brushed back from his forehead like a lion's mane, and his deeply tanned skin stretched over high cheekbones beneath those startlingly clear, light blue eyes, was distinctly sinister. In fact, the man in black was obviously a *very* nasty bit of work. And the sooner she managed to get out of this house, the better.

Her thoughts were interrupted by a loud knock on the door, and she watched as a man in a brown chauffeur's uniform entered the room.

'I'm sorry to interrupt you, Mr Smith-Farrell, but it's time we were setting off for the House of Lords.'

With his back to her, the man in black failed to notice Kate's startled jump, or the fact that she was now sitting bolt upright, and staring at him with horrified eyes.

Oh, no! On top of everything else—this was just *too much*! Surely he couldn't possibly be...? Maybe she hadn't heard his name correctly?

'Just a moment, Horace,' the man told the chauffeur as he strode quickly back to the desk and picked up the telephone once more. This time, unfortunately, Kate had no difficulty at all in hearing exactly what he was saying.

'Ah, Mr Armstrong...? Yes, it's Dominic Smith-Farrell here. I'm afraid there's been an accident to my car...yes, it looks like a total write-off, I'm afraid. In fact, it was a deliberate action carried out by a third party. And, while I rather think it comes under the heading of malicious damage, I'm not sure of the exact position as far as my insurance policy is concerned.'

Oh, lord! Kate could feel the blood draining from her face. She had been intending to visit her widowed aunt Laura in a few days' time, before beginning her tour of Europe. Well, that plan was now definitely off! How could life be so unfair? What a really dreadful accident of fate, that she might possibly be meeting one of her cousins, right now—and in such *awful* circumstances! Oh, help— what on earth was she going to do?

'. . . Thank you, Mr Armstrong. I'll be in touch.' Dominic Smith-Farrell put down the receiver and turned to face her. 'Well, the good news is that I appear to be fully covered for what my insurance agent confirms is a case of malicious damage,' he drawled, giving her a cold sardonic smile. 'However, the bad news—certainly as far as *you* are concerned—is that, irrespective of any police action taken against you, my insurance company will be suing you for the full cost of a new car.'

'That's no problem,' she assured him hurriedly. 'I really am *very* sorry to have caused so much damage—and I'll be happy to pay whatever it costs for your automobile to be replaced.'

'Oh, really. . . ?' He raised a dark eyebrow, pausing for a moment before naming a sum which made Kate gasp with horror.

'You've got to be kidding!'

'Oh, no, I'm not,' he assured her, with what she thought of as unnecessary relish. 'Do you have that amount of money here in England?'

'Not all of it, no. But I guess I could get in touch with my trustees in Canada, and . . .'

The hateful man gave a bark of caustic laughter. 'Oh, no, I'm not falling for that old trick! Frankly, I don't believe you've got two pennies to rub together,' he said, viewing her cement-splattered clothes with contempt, before turning to the chauffeur, who had remained standing silently by the door.

'All right, Horace. I can't wait here all day for the police to turn up, so I suggest that you bring the Rolls around to the front door. It now seems that we'll be going to the House of Lords via the local police station.'

Despite riding through the streets of London in a luxurious, chauffeur-driven Rolls-Royce, Kate was certain that she'd never felt so sick and frightened in all her born days.

'Please, won't you change your mind? Do we *really* have to get the police involved in this business?' she pleaded urgently to the man sitting beside her in the back of the vehicle. 'I know what I did was very wrong—but surely even *you* must have had a romance that didn't work out?'

'My past life is none of your concern,' he snapped curtly, his cheeks flushing beneath his tan as he quickly leaned forward to press a button, raising a glass partition which prevented his chauffeur from hearing any more of their conversation.

'But haven't you ever done something stupid, and then bitterly regretted it? Er... when you were very much younger, of course, I mean,' she added quickly as she saw his blue eyes flash with anger.

'I'm not exactly in my dotage!' he told her bitterly. 'In fact, I can tell you that I'm engaged to be married to a very beautiful, clever and delightful girl. And neither she nor I would ever dream of becoming involved in such a disgraceful escapade—or of causing a large amount of damage to another person's property,' he added in crushing tones as the Rolls came to a halt outside the police station.

'I reckon you're just about the pits!' Kate declared, throwing Dominic Smith-Farrell a glance of venomous dislike as he gripped her arm and led her inside the building.

'Well, Miss ... er ... Macaulay—if that really *is* your name?—I can't say it's been a pleasure meeting you, because it most certainly hasn't,' he drawled silkily, ignoring her harsh words. 'However, I have a very strong feeling that we will be meeting again—in court.'

'I'm very sorry I damaged your car,' Kate retorted angrily. 'But now I've had the misfortune to meet you, I can only say that I'm simply amazed that nobody's done it to you before now!'

'Oh, really?' he grated, an angry muscle beating in his clenched jaw.

'And how you *ever* managed to find someone willing to marry you completely beats me,' she added nastily, as a policeman prepared to take down her statement. 'Quite frankly, I'd rather be shacked up with Bluebeard or Ivan the Terrible any day!'

'And you'd certainly deserve them both!' he retorted with a grim bark of laughter, before turning on his heel and striding back out into the street.

Oh, yes, Kate thought as she now drove slowly down the long, winding avenue of ancient oak trees, towards the huge Jacobean mansion whose large, mullioned bow windows shimmered and sparkled in the afternoon sun, there was no doubt that Dominic Smith-Farrell was a *thoroughly* detestable man.

In fact, the only crumb of comfort in the whole unpleasant affair was the knowledge that he must have been absolutely furious when that nice, kindly old magistrate had dismissed the case against her.

Kate couldn't help grinning at the thought of Dominic's rage and fury, before reminding herself that she'd had to pay a very high price for her foolish action in damaging his car. Finding the money to pay his insurance company hadn't been easy. The loss of funds had meant curtailing her tour of Europe, and she was definitely going to have to get some sort of job here in England, to enable her to buy a plane ticket home to Canada.

However, at least her trip to Norfolk this weekend should be free of any trouble. She hated to think what would have happened if she'd turned up here, at Thornton Priory, to find Dominic spreading doom and gloom at her first meeting with the other members of his family. Thank goodness the horrid man was many thousands of miles away, in Hong Kong!

CHAPTER TWO

As SHE neared the end of the great avenue of oak trees, Kate brought her vehicle to a halt. Her gaze moved past the old stone bridge over a fast-running stream and on to where Thornton Priory lay in a secluded hollow, surrounded by wide green lawns.

Looking at the immensely impressive, huge stone building, Kate shook her head with astonishment. It was colossal! How could anyone possibly afford to live in a place like this? As far as she knew, Aunt Laura and her husband had not been at all well off. And yet the cost of keeping the fabric of this building in good repair must be astronomical. As for the heating bills . . . !

Her thoughts were interrupted by the steady pounding of hoofbeats, and she turned to see a horse and rider approaching behind her.

'I say——' the rider called out, 'I hope you won't mind my saying so, but I'm afraid you're trespassing on private property.'

Kate looked up at the boy on the horse, who was now showing far more interest in her vehicle than in the fact that she might be a trespasser.

'Yes, I know this is private property. However, Mrs Smith-Farrell has invited me to stay for a few days,' Kate explained as she removed her black helmet, allowing the long mass of tawny-coloured hair to flow down over her black leather jacket.

'Oh, well, that's all right, then.' The boy turned his head to gaze with frank longing at her large motorcycle. 'That looks a terrific machine! Does it go very fast?'

'Um...yes, it does!' She smiled up at the boy, who appeared to be about seventeen or eighteen years of age. 'But I reckon we ought to introduce ourselves, because I guess you must be one of my cousins.'

He frowned, patting his horse's neck as the animal moved restlessly beneath him. 'I don't think...' He paused for a moment, looking down at her doubtfully. 'My mother did say something about "dear little Katherine" coming to stay with us. But that description doesn't seem to fit you, somehow,' he added with youthful candour, grinning down at the tall, well-built girl sitting so casually astride the enormous motorcycle.

'No, I'm afraid it doesn't!' she laughed. 'But that's exactly who I am—although I prefer to be known as Kate. And you are...?'

'My name's Martin,' the boy replied, gazing with increasing longing at the sleek lines of her large machine. 'I say, can I ride with you down to the house?'

'Sure you can,' she said. 'But what about your horse?'

Martin gave a whoop of delight. 'That's no problem,' he said, quickly leaping to the ground and dragging the horse over to a nearby tree, where he tied its bridle to one of the lower branches. 'I've wanted a fast motorbike for simply ages, but old Dom has always refused to buy me one.'

It sounded as if 'old Dom' was capable of being just as disagreeable here in Norfolk as he had been in London, Kate thought grimly. Once again she thanked her lucky stars that the dreadful man was far away in Hong Kong.

'Here, you'd better put this on,' she said, twisting around to hand Martin her helmet as she tried to remember the family set-up which her aunt had rattled off at the end of her phone call. As far as Kate could recall, apart from the hateful Dominic— who was obviously very much older than his half-brother and sister—Martin was almost eighteen and he had a younger sister, Alice, who must be about sixteen. However, she would soon be able to sort them all out, she decided, and in the meantime she was clearly going to have her work cut out convincing Martin that motorcycles were potentially dangerous machines.

'Do I really have to wear this?' he asked, pulling a face as she jammed the heavy helmet down on his head.

'Yes, you do,' she replied firmly. 'It's mad not to wear one—besides being thoroughly illegal not to do so—and I'm not prepared to risk having anything happen to you while you're on my machine. So quit arguing, huh?'

'OK, let's roll, baby!' he retorted with a wide grin as he mimicked her Canadian accent.

Kate laughed. 'If you wanna ride, you'd better button up your lip, kid!' she growled in her best imitation of Al Capone, before turning back to switch on the ignition.

Their arrival at Thornton Priory caused quite a commotion. The sound of the powerful thousand c.c. engine as the machine roared into the courtyard, together with Martin's wild yells of delight, seemed to bring people running from all directions.

Kate felt initially stunned and confused amid all the hubbub—the noise level further increased by wild barking, from what appeared to be a large pack of dogs. However, as the deafening clamour slowly began to subside, she gradually began to sort out the various members of the family.

She already knew Martin, of course, although she had no idea of who the elderly man in a black coat and striped trousers might be. However, the middle-aged lady standing in the open doorway, with wispy faded blonde hair escaping from an untidy knot on top of her head, could only be Aunt Laura.

'Hello, I'm Alice. I'm just crazy about all that black leather gear you're wearing. Can I try it on later?'

Kate turned to see a young girl standing beside her. Ye gods, Alice was *really* something else! she thought, her eyes widening at the sight of the girl's long black lace dress covered in a heavily fringed black shawl, the large black felt hat, whose acid green ostrich feathers exactly matched the colour painted on her long fingernails, and the extraordinary bizarre make-up on the girl's face, repeating the same frightful combination of black and green.

'I feel like a change of style. I'm rather tired of being a Gothic,' Alice explained. 'So I thought I'd move into the Heavy Metal scene. That black leather outfit of yours would be perfect.'

'Yes, well, I guess it would at that,' Kate muttered, momentarily disconcerted by the girl's weird appearance.

'You will let me borrow your clothes, won't you?' Alice said urgently.

Kate gave a helpless shrug. 'Yes, sure, of course.'

'Really, Alice, do stop being such a nuisance!' the faded blonde woman called out as Kate dismounted from the machine and made her way across the gravel towards her aunt, standing beneath the huge, ornately carved stone porch.

'My dear little Katherine!' Laura Smith-Farrell breathed. The older woman was obviously still clutching feebly at the fast-vanishing picture of the small niece she remembered. Raising her face to gaze up at the girl towering above her, she whispered tremulously, 'How lovely to see you. So happy...so like your dear father...poor Tom!'

Emerging from her aunt's embrace, and about to follow her inside the house, Kate turned back to survey the milling scene in the courtyard. She still hadn't been introduced to the elderly man, but other than that extraordinary young girl, Alice—and it was impossible to tell what she looked like beneath all that awful make-up!—the members of her new family seemed to bear a very close resemblance to one another. Like their mother, both her cousins had light fair hair. So how come Dominic was so dark? Her thoughts were interrupted as Martin asked if he could put her motorbike away in the garage.

'Sure you can. Or take it for a run, if you want to,' she called out to him.

Martin gave a shout of glee and quickly jumped astride the machine, with Alice clambering up on the pillion seat behind him. As he switched on the powerful engine, she could now see that the 'pack' of dogs—who were once again barking their heads off—comprised three black Labradors and what looked like an elderly Irish wolfhound.

'Do come inside, Katherine,' her aunt murmured, leading the way through the porch and into the hall of Thornton Priory. 'I'm sure you'd like a cup of tea . . . just the thing after a long journey. But I don't think you've met Osborne, have you?' she added, turning to the elderly man who had followed them into the hall.

'I'm pleased to meet you, Mr Osborne,' Kate smiled, wondering just how he fitted into the family as she shook the elderly man's hand.

'Just Osborne, if you don't mind,' he replied firmly. 'And if I may say so, it's very pleasant to meet you again, Miss Katherine. I remember your father very well. A most charming gentleman,' he added gravely, before telling her aunt Laura that he would be serving tea in the drawing-room.

'That would be very nice, Osborne,' the older woman agreed as she took her niece's arm and led her across the great hall—one of the most beautiful rooms Kate had ever seen.

'Goodness, you've even got a minstrels' gallery!' she exclaimed, stopping to gaze up at the barrel-vault ceiling, arching two storeys high above her head, whose wooden beams bore carvings of Tudor roses picked out in gold leaf. The walls of the room, which had to be at least fifty feet long, were covered in dark oak panelling, the same oak forming a handsome, carved surround to the mammoth fireplace—which seemed big enough to burn even the largest logs.

'Yes, it is lovely. Luckily, this side of the house wasn't damaged when the house caught fire,' Aunt Laura said as she opened a door in the far end of the hall.

'How awful! Did you lose many possessions?' Kate asked as they entered a large sitting-room, whose curved, mullioned bow windows she had seen when first approaching the Priory.

'Oh, no, dear. It all happened long ago, before I married dear Hector. Poor Dominic's mother... such a very beautiful Spanish girl. Unfortunately, she was overcome by the smoke and fumes. So terribly young to die, don't you think?' The older woman sighed heavily as she sank down into an open chair.

Kate looked at her with startled eyes. 'I didn't know—I mean, I didn't realise...'

'Yes,' her aunt sighed again. 'Such a tragic loss, and so very, very sad for poor Dominic. Ah, here's Osborne with a nice cup of tea,' she added as the elderly man came into the room carrying a heavy tray.

'I've put another kettle on to boil, because you may need some more hot water, madam,' he told her aunt, setting out plates of cucumber sandwiches and a large fruit cake.

'Dear Osborne, I don't know *what* we'd do without him,' Aunt Laura sighed as he left the room. 'He's getting a bit long in the tooth now, of course, and having a butler is such an anachronism in this day and age, isn't it?' she continued as she cut a slice of cake and handed it to Kate. 'However, since he's a much better cook than I am,' she added with a breathless laugh, 'I've absolutely refused to allow him to retire.'

'Well, if he made this fruit cake, I must say I absolutely agree with you,' Kate said enthusiastically as she greedily helped herself to another slice. 'I'm afraid I don't have any memories of my first visit here, when I was just a young kid. Has Osborne been with you for a long time?'

'Oh, goodness, yes. He was here at the Priory long before I married dear Hector,' the older woman told her as she picked up a large silver teapot. 'That's why I'm so pleased he's agreed to come with me and the children when we move into the Dower House.'

Kate frowned in puzzlement. 'But surely—I mean, you and your children live *here*, don't you? Why would you want to leave this lovely house? Of course, I know it's huge—and obviously a terrific problem to heat in the winter—but it's your home, isn't it?'

Aunt Laura, who had been speaking perfectly normally since entering the room, suddenly reverted to her breathless, jumbled conversation, which left Kate feeling almost as breathless and confused as her aunt.

'Oh, yes, Katherine, very happy here... but in the circumstances... Dominic's marriage, you see? Quite the usual thing in England... the family leaving to make way for the new wife. And Helen... lovely girl, of course... so suitable... quite perfect. But the children are at an awkward age... difficult situation, you see...?'

Unfortunately, Kate didn't see. However, when her aunt became suddenly very agitated, begging her niece not to say anything to Dominic about the rest of the family's plans, Kate was happy to reassure the older woman that she wouldn't dream of saying a word. 'My lips are sealed,' Kate assured her aunt solemnly.

'Thank you, dear. I...I wouldn't like you to think...Dominic and I...always *very* fond of one another. But it's not the right time, just now. He was so terribly cross with Martin, for having that nasty argument and being so rude to Helen. Although I really can't see any harm in the Living History people coming here, can you?'

Kate gave a sympathetic murmur of agreement, while wondering what on earth her aunt was talking about. The 'Living History people'? Who were they supposed to be?

It obviously wasn't possible for her to tell her aunt that she was only staying here at the Priory because Dominic was abroad. And, since she didn't feel she could cope with much more of this disjointed type of conversation, Kate quickly decided to change the subject.

'If you don't mind, Aunt Laura, I would prefer not to be called Katherine. I did try to warn you on the phone that I've grown more than somewhat since we last met,' she said with a rueful laugh. 'Quite honestly, I think my father was quite right when he said that plain Kate suited me much better. And let's face it...' she grinned '...I'm afraid that in my case, big is not exactly beautiful!'

Her niece was quite right, the elderly woman thought. 'Beautiful' wasn't the right word for this very tall girl, with her long tawny-coloured hair and wide, sparkling blue eyes fringed by thick black lashes. However, even she could see that her niece possessed a warm, magnetic personality—a charismatic attraction which far outstripped mere beauty. There was no doubt that, having once met Kate, you would never be able to forget her.

'Well, of course, dear, I'll be happy to call you Kate, if that's what you want. And we must have a long talk about your poor dear father...' Her aunt paused, turning her head and wincing at the sound of an angry bellow, which was swiftly followed by the noise of hard, firm footsteps approaching across the stone floor of the hall.

A moment later the door of the large sitting-room was thrown open.

'I want to know what's going on, Laura!' a man demanded as he strode into the room. 'I've just seen Martin, with Alice sitting up behind him, and looking more like a witch than ever, careering around the park on a gigantic motorbike. I thought I'd already made it absolutely clear that I don't approve of such dangerous vehicles?'

'Yes, dear, of course you have,' the older woman agreed soothingly. 'But I'm sure they've only gone for a short ride on Kate's machine.'

'Whose machine?' He frowned, before turning to catch his first glimpse of the girl sitting in a large armchair. 'Good lord! What on earth are *you* doing here?'

Completely paralysed with shock, Kate was unable to say or do anything other than stare up at the tall man with her mind in a complete whirl. Dominic Smith-Farrell? Here in Norfolk? But surely... surely he was supposed to be in Hong Kong?

'Dominic dear, that's hardly the way to greet your new cousin!' Aunt Laura gave a nervous laugh, bestowing an apologetic smile on the girl who was looking quite stunned by her stepson's abrupt entry into the room. 'Dear Cousin Kate has come to stay with us for a few days... isn't that nice?' she continued, picking up the silver teapot. 'So why don't you make her feel welcome... get to know each other... while I ask Osborne to make a fresh pot of tea?'

In any other circumstances, Kate might have found the sight of the appalled, horrified expression on Dominic's face extremely funny. As it was, however, her sense of humour seemed to have completely deserted her. Her mind numb with shock from his totally unexpected appearance, she remained sitting dazed and frozen in her chair as her aunt left the room.

The long silence following the older woman's departure was almost deafening. At last, after closing his eyes for a moment and taking a deep breath, Dominic succeeded in pulling himself together.

'What in the hell are you doing here? Is this some sort of ghastly joke?' he demanded angrily. 'You're certainly no cousin of mine!'

'No... er... you're quite right,' Kate croaked, managing to find her voice at last.

'Well, in that case——'

'No, you don't understand,' she muttered, still trying to come to terms with the full horror of the situation. 'I'm not *your* cousin, but I am theirs...'

She waved her hand feebly in the air. 'I—I mean, Martin and Alice, your half-brother and -sister.'

'I simply don't believe it!' he grated, his icy-blue eyes sweeping over her long, slim legs clothed in black leather trousers, topped by a matching leather jacket. 'I refuse to believe that any of us could possibly be related to a girl dressed like...like some sort of Hell's Angel!' he exploded angrily.

'Well, that's just too bad!' she retorted, scowling up at the loathsome man. 'Because your stepmother *is* my aunt, and losing your temper—not to mention being so rude—isn't going to alter the fact.'

He glared down at her, a muscle beating frantically in his clenched jaw as he fought to control his fury. And then, swearing violently under his breath, he strode across the room to stand with his back to her as he stared silently out of the window for some moments.

'All right, Miss Macaulay,' he growled in a low, menacing voice as he turned around to face her once more. 'Let's begin again, shall we? And to start with—I want to know what you're doing here.'

But Kate, who had used the break in Dominic's interrogation to pull herself together, lifted her chin defiantly towards him. 'That's the question I was going to ask *you*!' she told him bitterly. 'I thought you were supposed to be in Hong Kong?'

'The case has been delayed,' he said, pushing an irritated hand through his dark hair. 'But that has nothing to do with...'

'Oh, yes, it has!' she snapped. 'I'd never have come within a million miles of this place if I'd known you were going to be here!'

'Well, the solution is perfectly obvious.' He gave a harsh bark of laughter. 'Why don't you just hop on to that machine of yours—I take it that huge motorcycle really *does* belong to you?—and buzz off?'

Kate glared mutinously up at him. 'Why should I? Aunt Laura has invited me to be her guest for the weekend, and——'

'Good lord! Are you trying to tell me you really *are* some sort of cousin?'

'Yes, of course I am!' she retorted curtly. 'Your stepmother—who also happens to be my aunt Laura—is my father's only sister. Or was, I suppose I should say, since Dad died some three years ago,' she added as he stared down at her with a blank expression on his face.

'Then you must be...oh no!' he groaned. 'It never occurred to me that my stepmother's niece, "dear little Katherine Macaulay", could possibly be the same great hulk of a girl, the Miss Macaulay who poured cement all over my car!'

'Who are you calling a great hulk?' Kate demanded furiously.

'Yes, well, I—I'm sorry. I shouldn't have said that,' he muttered, a dark flush rising over his handsome, tanned features.

'I know I'm tall,' Kate fumed. 'But there's no need to——'

'I've already apologised,' he snapped. 'In fact, if it makes you feel any better, I'm prepared to admit that you are obviously very attractive....'

'Gee whizz, thanks a bunch!'

'...And, at your trial, you certainly managed to charm the magistrate half out of his wits. Even my own solicitor had the gall to tell me—*me*, the injured party!—that he wouldn't mind getting his hands on you,' Dominic added sourly.

Kate looked at him with open-mouthed astonishment for a moment, then burst out laughing. 'Wow! If that's your idea of a compliment, I'll pass!'

'Oh, hell, I didn't mean——'

'I'm really *very* surprised at you, Dominic,' she told him sternly, trying to keep her face straight, and hiding the glee she felt at having wrong-footed the horrid man. 'I thought you were supposed to be such a smooth, sophisticated London lawyer?'

'Yes, and so I am—in *normal* circumstances,' he retorted through clenched teeth. 'But having to deal with you, you frightful girl, is enough to try the patience of a saint!'

She gave him a tight, malicious smile. 'Oh, dear! Never mind, maybe I'll grow on you, in time?'

He responded to her words with a grim laugh, before he turned and began pacing restlessly up and down the room. 'I realise I can't throw you out of this house immediately. However...'

'Hey, come on! Let's relax, huh?' Kate interjected quickly. 'It's pretty stupid for the two of us to be standing here trading insults with one another. OK, I'll admit that you had every right to be absolutely furious at what I did to your car. But that was well over three months ago. I settled in full with the insurance company, right? So why all the grief now?' she asked.

'I don't expect you to understand—but you succeeded in making me the laughing stock of my profession,' he told her bitterly. 'I'm still trying to live down that headline in the London *Evening Standard*: "Lawyer in Revenge Drama",' he added gloomily.

'Oh, dear...' muttered Kate, trying hard to keep her face straight. It didn't look as if Dominic had much of a sense of humour—certainly none as far as that unfortunate court case was concerned. 'Look, if it will help matters, I'm quite prepared to explain everything to your family,' she offered. 'And I'll stress the fact that I behaved very badly towards you. So...'

'*No!*' he retorted quickly. 'There's no need...er...I mean, there's no point in digging up the unfortunate affair again, is there?'

Kate stared up at his tall, rigid figure. What was going on? Why, after all Dominic's rage and fury, didn't he want her to make a grovelling apology, and tell everyone it was all her fault? Unless...?

'You...you haven't told your family about what happened to your car, have you?' she said slowly. And then she realised that she had hit the nail sharply on the head, as once again she watched a dark flush rising up over his handsome features.

'No, you awful girl, I haven't!' he hissed through clenched teeth. 'It was bad enough having to put up with my colleagues' jibes and laughter: "Hello, Dominic—seen any large cement trucks lately?"' he mimicked acidly. 'I certainly didn't need my stepmother or my young brother and sister joining in the general hilarity and mirth.'

'But what about the girl you're going to marry? Surely she must know all about it?'

'Helen was away on business at the time—in America,' he retorted curtly.

'Ho! I see it all now. It's a case of injured male pride. Your macho image, right?'

'Nonsense!'

'Oh, yeah?' She gave him a wide, cynical smile as she eased herself comfortably back in her chair. 'Well, you can relax.'

'Ah, I see you've decided to be sensible. When are you planning to leave?' he asked hopefully, his lips tightening as she slowly shook her head.

'No, I'm not going. Why should I?'

Dominic gave a snort of grim laughter. 'I can think of a few good reasons. How about, If you don't leave tomorrow, I'm going to be making your life *extremely* uncomfortable?'

'Oh, no, you won't,' she told him confidently. 'Because what we've got going here is a stand-off situation.'

'I've no idea what you're talking about.'

She gave a dramatic sigh. 'I thought you were supposed to be so clever?'

'*Kate!* I warn you, don't try my patience too far,' he growled.

'Hey, cool it, man! There's no need to get excited,' she murmured soothingly. 'It's all very simple. *I* will promise not to tell anyone about the dastardly deed which I performed on your car. And in return, *you're* going to welcome your stepmother's niece into this house with open arms.'

He glared angrily at her. 'That's nothing more or less than blackmail!'

'No—really?' Kate airily brushed an invisible speck of dust off the arm of her black leather jacket. 'Well, of course you're the legal eagle around here. But it sounds like a fair bargain to me.'

'I bet it does,' he grated.

'Well, do we have a deal?' she murmured as they heard the sound of dogs barking, and the approaching click of high heels on the stone floor of the hall.

Dominic glared at her with acute dislike. 'It looks as though you've got me over a barrel just at the moment. But don't make the mistake of thinking I'm going to let you get away with this!' he added in a savage undertone as her aunt entered the room.

'Here I am at last,' she informed them, putting the freshly made pot of tea and an extra cup down on the tray. 'I didn't mean to be so long, but the fishmonger suddenly arrived, and . . .'

'I'm sorry, Laura, but I'm afraid I can't stop for a cup of tea,' Dominic said, glancing down at his watch. 'I've got to meet Helen off the London train.'

'Of course, dear, I'd forgotten she was coming to stay with us for the weekend. Her father, the general, told me that with all those builders in his house Helen would be far more comfortable here. It will be so . . . er . . . nice for Kate to meet your fiancée,' his stepmother added as he walked towards the door, before she turned to her niece. 'I do hope dear Dominic has been making you feel welcome?'

'Oh, goodness me, yes—*dear* Dominic has been absolutely peachy-dreamy!' Kate cooed, giving his suddenly stiff, rigid figure a wide beaming smile, which she hoped he would find profoundly irritating. 'In fact, he's just begged me to stay here at the Priory for as long as I like. Right, Dominic?'

For one awful moment Kate thought he was going to explode with suppressed fury. However, with what was clearly a massive effort, he managed to bring himself under control.

'Kate is quite right,' he told his stepmother through gritted teeth. 'Unfortunately, your dear niece tells me she can only manage to stay with us for the weekend. Right, Kate?'

Oh-oh! He'd really thrown the gauntlet down now, hadn't he? Kate stiffened her backbone and took a deep breath.

'Yes, I was thinking of leaving on Monday. But Dominic has made me feel *so* welcome that I've decided to change my mind. After all, what could be nicer than to spend a few weeks in the beautiful English countryside?'

And let's see how you get yourself out of *that* one, buster! she thought silently as she gave him a wide, artless smile.

Unfortunately, it seemed that the hateful man was as slippery as an eel.

'How remiss of me—I should have realised you would want to see as much of the English country-side as possible,' he told her, accompanying his words with a glance of pure poison. 'So, first thing on Monday morning, I'll arrange for you to go on a long-distance coach tour of the British Isles.'

'There's no need for you to bother...' Kate muttered quickly, realising that it looked as if once again she had been out-manoeuvred by Dominic Smith-Farrell.

'Nonsense! I can assure you it will give me nothing but the deepest pleasure to pay for your ticket,' he drawled smoothly, giving her a bland and quite maddening smile before turning to leave the room, and closing the door very quietly behind him.

CHAPTER THREE

KATE stared out of the open casement window, her wide blue eyes barely registering the sheep grazing in the park, or the late afternoon sun sparkling on the far distant fields of ripening corn.

This visit to Norfolk, to meet up with her long-lost family, was turning out to be a real can of worms! So OK, it was rotten luck to find Dominic here at Thornton Priory, and not safely miles away in Hong Kong. But why hadn't she possessed the basic sense to telephone her aunt this morning, just to check that the coast was clear? And that wasn't the only mistake she'd made, was it?

What a prize fool you are, she told herself, sighing heavily as she turned around to survey the large room. With its massive oak four-poster bed with heavily embroidered silk drapes, and the large faded tapestries hanging on the walls, it was just the sort of bedroom for which she would normally have given her eye-teeth to sleep in. But in her present circumstances...? Kate sighed again. What on earth had possessed her to challenge Dominic—practically forcing him to let her stay on here, at the Priory?

Even if she didn't like the idea of anyone being able to push her around—and she most certainly didn't!—that really was no excuse for her having so quickly picked up the gauntlet thrown down by the horrid man. Her friend Jayne had warned her about being far too impulsive. 'You're a super, kind, warm-hearted girl, Kate—but why do you always have to dash in where angels fear to tread?'

Jayne had been quite right, of course. After all, this was Dominic's house, and since she'd obviously caused him the maximum amount of embarrassment when she had damaged his car Kate couldn't entirely blame him for wanting to get rid of her, *tout de suite*. And that was a real pity, because this old house looked really fascinating, and her new cousins appeared to be an interesting bunch of characters. She'd definitely taken a shine to Martin, although she wasn't at all sure about his sister Alice. As far as she could see, that young girl was really very weird—definitely freaky-deaky! And her aunt Laura seemed to be acting in a strange manner as well. Not only did the older woman appear to be extraordinarily nervous and twitchy, but her conversation was more like double-Dutch than English.

Kate had heard all about English eccentricity. However, she was quite sure that some reason, or some problem, must lie behind both Aunt Laura's and Alice's odd behaviour. So it was a real shame that Dominic seemed intent on kicking her out of the Priory as soon as possible. And there wasn't much she could do about that, Kate told herself as she glanced down at her watch, realising that she was going to have to get a move on if she was intending to have a bath and change before dinner.

In normal circumstances, maybe she and Dominic might have been able to be friends. Unfortunately, not only had she inadvertently destroyed his car—why did men seem to have this 'thing' about their automobiles?—but he obviously couldn't stand her, personally, either. And that was just fine, Kate thought with a dismissive shrug of her shoulders as she walked through into the small bathroom. Because she had never, in all her born days, met anyone *quite* so rude and aggressive as Dominic Smith-Farrell. And how he'd ever managed to persuade someone to marry him was completely beyond her. His fiancée must be an absolute saint to put up with that man's diabolical personality!

After towelling herself dry, Kate left the adjacent small bathroom, with its old-fashioned tub and antiquated plumbing. Walking back into the bedroom, she frowned at the dress hanging on the outside of the wardrobe. She had always believed in travelling light, and on her recent tour around Europe, on the back of the second-hand motorcycle which she had bought in Germany, Kate hadn't had much choice in the matter. So, when packing the bare essentials for what she'd assumed would be a quiet weekend in the Norfolk countryside, it had never occurred to her that she might be expected to dress for dinner. It wouldn't be a problem, tomorrow, to zip into the nearest town and buy something more suitable. But, here and now, all she had to wear was that skimpy dress which she had thrown into her case at the last minute.

Standing in front of the mirror some time later, Kate could only shrug with resignation. There was no doubt that the black silky garment, primarily designed to be worn on a beach over her bikini, was thoroughly unsuitable for an English dining-room.

And, from the way the low-cut, sleeveless and *very* short dress clung to her generous curves, it was only going to underline Dominic's description of her as a 'great hulk', she thought glumly. What a swine the man was!

Attempting to pull up the front of her dress, hoping to cover the deep cleft between her breasts, while at the same time trying to tug the short skirt down towards her knees, Kate gave up the unequal struggle as she heard a knock on the door.

'Hi there,' she smiled at Alice as the girl popped her head around the door.

'My mother asked me to come up and see how you're getting on,' Alice said, coming into the room. 'I hope she told you about the plumbing in your bathroom? Did she explain that hot water only comes out of the cold tap?'

Kate laughed. 'No, unfortunately she didn't. But it's quite OK, because it only took me a few minutes to work it out.'

Trying not to stare too obviously at the young girl, Kate was relieved to see that Alice had removed most of her frightful make-up. She was still wearing those ghastly clothes, of course. However, now that she could clearly see the girl's face and her long, pale gold hair tied up in a neat ponytail, she thought that Alice was definitely looking a whole lot better. In fact, Kate told herself, if the kid would only give herself a chance, she might turn out to be a real beauty.

'It isn't the plumbing in this house which is proving to be a problem,' Kate told her gloomily. 'It's what I'm going to wear tonight which is giving me such a headache.'

'What on earth are you worried about? I think you look sensational!' Alice told her, enviously eyeing her new Canadian cousin's mane of sun-streaked, amber-coloured hair, and the short silk dress which clung to the older girl's magnificent body. 'I do wish I were as tall as you,' she sighed, gazing at the extraordinarily long, slim tanned legs, which seemed to start from somewhere beneath Kate's shoulders.

'Dominic said I was a great hulk of a girl,' Kate muttered. 'And I guess he was right, at that,' she added, grimacing at herself in the mirror. A second later, her cheeks flushed as she guiltily recalled that she wasn't supposed to have met Alice's half-brother before her arrival at the Priory this after-noon. Even Dominic—just about the rudest man she'd ever known—was unlikely to be quite so im-polite towards someone he apparently hadn't met before.

However, Alice didn't appear to have noticed anything out of the ordinary about her brother's remark—which must say volumes about his abrasive personality!—as she wandered aimlessly about the room.

'I must admit that I'm a bit fed up with old Dom at the moment,' the younger girl confided. 'But he's normally very kind and helpful—even when Martin and I are quite obviously driving him up the wall. So I expect he was only teasing you.'

Kate stared at her in astonishment. Dominic—kind and helpful...? Not as far as she was con-cerned, he wasn't! His sister ought to know what she was talking about. But since every time Kate had seen the awful man he'd been breathing rage and fury, she seriously wondered if they were talking about the same person.

She looked up to see that the other girl was still wandering around the large bedroom, aimlessly picking up various items of clothing and holding them up against herself, before putting them down again with a heavy sigh. Kate was no psychologist, but even she could see that Alice appeared to be deeply troubled about something.

'I don't want to step out of line...' Kate apologised. 'However, if you don't mind my saying so, you don't seem to be exactly brimming over with the joys of spring. Is there anything I can do to help?'

'No, not really.' The girl gave a heavy, dramatic sigh. 'Well, the fact is...' She hesitated for a moment. 'I expect everyone else is bound to tell you, so I might as well put you in the picture myself. The fact is, I've just been expelled from my school.'

'Expelled? Whatever for?' Kate looked at her in surprise. 'Did you do something really diabolical?'

'No—I only wish, now, that I had,' the younger girl told her gloomily. 'As soon as I'd finished my GCSE exams, I was chucked out and told not to go back.'

'I'm all ears,' Kate grinned. 'What on earth did you do?'

'I was sacked for wearing what the headmistress called "outrageous clothes and make-up",' Alice muttered glumly. 'Honestly, some grown-ups are really *pathetic*, aren't they?'

Kate couldn't help feeling that the girl's headmistress had a point, but it would clearly be undiplomatic to say so.

'Yeah—well, life can be tough at times,' she murmured sympathetically. 'On the other hand, your clothes and make-up are possibly just a little...er...bizarre for a young girl. Of course,' she added quickly, 'I could be absolutely wrong. Maybe wearing outfits which would be perfect for a movie production of *I was a Teenage Vampire* is the latest fashion for kids, here in England...?'

Alice responded to her words with a surprising gurgle of laughter. 'No, it certainly isn't! And that's the whole point, you see? Unfortunately...' she gave another heavy sigh '...it doesn't look as if my plan is going to work.'

'Your plan...?'

'Oh, it's nothing very important,' Alice muttered, and Kate, who could well remember the pain and tribulation of being sixteen, quickly decided not to probe any further.

'OK, so why don't you tell me who's going to be downstairs for dinner tonight?' she asked, picking up a brush and dragging it through her long, tawny hair.

'Well, Ma, Dominic, Martin and myself, of course,' Alice told her. 'Then there's Helen— Dominic has just picked her up from the station— and her father, General Palmer, who lives in the next village, and...'

'Hey, hold it there!' Kate interjected quickly. 'Who's Helen? Is she the girl that's engaged to your brother Dominic?'

'Yes.'

She waited for a moment, but when Alice didn't elaborate on the subject, Kate asked impatiently, 'Well, what's Helen like?'

Alice stared at her with a blank expression for a moment, then shrugged. 'Helen? Well, she's very clever, of course, and holds down a terrifically important job in a bank in the City. She's also very beautiful and is always smiling; she never seems to lose her temper or...'

'Wow!' Kate exclaimed. 'Helen sounds an absolute paragon. I guess Dominic is really lucky to have found her, right?'

The younger girl hesitated for a moment, saved from having to reply by the deep, distant sound of a gong.

'Oops, it sounds as if everyone has arrived,' Alice exclaimed. 'And stop worrying—you look great!' she added, as she noticed Kate tugging at the short, tight skirt of her black dress. 'In fact...' she gave her new Canadian cousin a mischievous grin as they left the room and hurried down the wide oak staircase '...I bet Dominic is going to think you look absolutely terrific!'

Walking swiftly across the great hall, Kate didn't have the heart to tell Alice that she was quite wrong about Dominic's likely reaction. And, as they entered the large sitting-room, where the rest of the family and their guests were gathered, a quick glance at Dominic's tall figure instantly confirmed Kate's worst suspicions.

So OK, maybe Dominic didn't *exactly* faint with horror, but he nevertheless stood gazing at her with a stunned expression, as if he'd been hit by a very large sandbag. Closing his eyes for a moment, he took another dazed look at the display of so much of Kate's golden, tanned flesh, before turning away and pouring himself a very stiff drink. So who cares about him? Kate told herself defiantly, her confidence immediately restored as an elderly, distinguished-looking gentleman walked over to greet her.

'My dear girl, you're definitely a sight for sore eyes,' he said, giving her a broad smile and introducing himself as General Palmer. 'I knew your father, you know. It was many years ago, of course, but you're the spitting image of old Tom Macaulay. He was a devilishly handsome chap—women fell for him like ninepins!' the man added, gazing appreciatively at the tall girl in front of him. 'And I shouldn't be at all surprised if you don't have the same effect on young men nowadays.'

Kate laughed and shook her head. 'No, I'm not at all like my father. But thanks for the compliment.'

'Now see here, my boy,' the general called out to Dominic as he put an arm about Kate's waist, leading her across the room towards the drinks tray. 'How about some champagne for this perfectly splendid-looking girl?'

'Oh, no—please. I really don't drink very much alcohol,' Kate protested as Dominic turned a distinctly chilly eye in her direction.

'Nonsense! It's just the thing for you,' the elderly man told her, reaching across and lifting a large open bottle from a silver ice bucket. 'And I wouldn't mind having some myself either,' he grinned, handing the bottle to Dominic.

'There's really no need...' Kate protested.

'Rubbish—the boy can well afford it. And he has to be nice to me, because I'm his godfather.' The general winked at Kate. 'Right, Dominic?'

'Absolutely right, sir,' Dominic laughed, pouring the sparkling liquid into two tall, flute-shaped glasses and handing one to the general.

He was just holding out the other glass towards Kate when it was deftly seized by long, slim fingers and placed firmly down on the tray as a cool voice said, 'Really, Daddy! You mustn't badger the poor girl. Especially since alcoholism is so much on the increase nowadays.'

Kate, who hadn't known whether to be more surprised by the unexpected sight of Dominic's relaxed laughter or by the swift disappearance of her champagne glass, turned to face the woman standing beside her.

'We haven't met,' the elegant, dark-haired girl gave her a calm, composed smile, which didn't somehow seem to be reflected in her dark eyes. 'However, we will undoubtedly get to know each other very well, because I'm engaged to your step-cousin Dominic.'

Kate didn't have the opportunity to reply as the general took her arm and steered her away to meet the other guest, who had been invited to join the family for dinner.

'You'll have plenty of opportunity to natter to my daughter later, especially since she's staying here with Dominic for the weekend. We've got the builders into our house—the place is a dreadful mess,' he explained, introducing her to a stocky, thick-set man dressed in a hairy tweed suit.

George Wakeham apparently worked for a well-known firm of land agents. 'Good at his job, but a bit of a dull sort of chap,' the general whispered in her ear as George limply shook her hand, staring goggle-eyed at the tall girl's display of so much tanned flesh.

The general had been quite right—the land agent appeared to be as dull as ditchwater, Kate thought, sighing inwardly a few minutes later as Osborne announced that dinner was ready, and she found herself placed next to the man she was rapidly coming to think of as 'boring George'.

While Martin, seated on her left, was busily occupied in pouring the wine, she sipped the deliciously creamy, cold watercress soup, and glanced through her eyelashes down the long oval table at Dominic's fiancée.

So this was the woman of whom he had spoken so highly when, over three months ago, he had dragged Kate off to the police station in his chauffeur-driven Rolls-Royce. Well, she had to admit that Alice was right. Helen Palmer certainly was stunningly beautiful.

Aged about twenty-nine or thirty, the woman was wearing a shimmering, deep red silk dress, which set off to perfection her pale alabaster skin and sleek black hair, drawn into a chignon at the back of her head. Her dark red lipstick exactly matched her dress, and with a single strand of pearls about her neck and matching pearl earrings, Helen's smooth elegance made Kate suddenly feel very gauche and unsophisticated.

'It's great to have you here, Kate,' Martin's voice cut into her thoughts as he sat down beside her. 'How long are you going to be able to stay with us?'

'Er...I don't know exactly. But not very long, I'm afraid,' she told him, recalling Dominic's dire threats earlier in the afternoon. In fact, it would probably be a miracle if she managed to stick around here at the Priory for the rest of the weekend.

'Oh, that's a pity,' Martin said with a frown. 'I had been hoping you'd be able to stay with us until after the Living History battle.'

'Sure, I'd love to—if I knew what it was!' Kate laughed. 'Your mother mentioned something about it, but I hadn't a clue what she was talking about.'

'Well, there are quite a few societies and associations of people interested in history, who organise mock Civil War battles outside big houses—and some stately homes—during the summer. Associations like the Sealed Knot and the English Civil War Society, for instance,' he explained. 'Their members take it all very seriously, and make a terrific effort to wear the correct clothes and armour of the period. Hordes of people turn up to watch the battle, and most of the money collected goes to charity.'

Kate smiled. 'It sounds fun.'

'Yes, well, it *would* have been fun, if Helen hadn't put a spoke in the wheel,' he grumbled, scowling down the table at Dominic's fiancée.

'I'm sorry, but I don't quite understand . . . ?'

Martin shrugged. 'An old school friend told me that the Living History Company—who are usually booked up years ahead—had just had a sudden cancellation. So I immediately thought, why not put a battle on here at the Priory? This house has a strong association with King Charles the First, and the large lawns and field in front of the house would be a perfect stage for the mock battle. Don't you agree?'

'Sure, why not?' Kate grinned at him. 'It sounds a great idea!'

'Exactly! And when I rang up Dominic in London, he said he didn't mind—providing there was no damage to the house or garden. And then Helen got involved.' Martin sighed heavily. 'She kept going on and on about the mess, and the noise. So, now that he's going to be away in Hong Kong, Dom has decided that Helen is right, after all.'

'That sounds a real shame,' Kate agreed. 'Has the battle been cancelled?'

'Just about,' he told her gloomily. 'Dominic's intending to phone the Living History people on Monday, and tell them to find another venue.'

'Maybe he'll change his mind?'

Martin shook his head. 'There's not much chance of that, I'm afraid. Unfortunately, I lost my temper with Helen, and told her a few home truths.' He glanced sheepishly at Kate. 'Actually, we didn't just quarrel about the mock battle. She will keep on nagging me about going to university, when she knows all I want to do is to stay here and help Dom to farm the estate.'

'There's nothing wrong in wanting to do that,' Kate assured the boy, who was plainly very depressed about the whole affair. 'I grew up on a farm, and I'd be there still if my father hadn't left such a load of debts when he died.'

'It's all I've ever wanted to do,' Martin said enthusiastically, then gave a helpless shrug. 'Anyway, it was stupid of me to have a row with Helen. It didn't achieve anything, and after she'd complained about it to my brother, he was furiously angry with me as well. So...' Martin added with a sigh, 'as far as the Civil War battle is concerned, it looks as if I've made a real mess of things, doesn't it?'

'I'm sorry,' said Kate, gazing down the table at Helen, watching as the sleek, sophisticated woman smiled charmingly up into Dominic's eyes.

Kate knew she didn't have a lot of experience in these matters. However, she couldn't help thinking that if Martin—who obviously didn't like his brother's fiancée—was pinning his hopes on a broken engagement, he was likely to be disappointed. It was plain to see from the slanting glances, the intimate and possessive touch of her fingers on Dominic's arm, that Helen was declaring quite clearly: this man belongs to me.

And good luck to her! Kate thought grimly as Dominic bent his dark, arrogant head towards his fiancée. As far as she was concerned, getting married to that cold fish Dominic Smith-Farrell would definitely be a fate worse than death!

Looking back on the meal later, Kate decided that it was possibly unfortunate that 'boring George' Wakeham, who'd been sitting silently beside her, should have at this point decided to introduce a new topic of conversation.

'I say, Dominic,' he called out as Osborne began serving the guests with some delicious lamb cutlets, 'how are the plans for that Civil War battle coming along? Should be a jolly good show. What do you think, General?'

General Palmer, who clearly hadn't gained high rank in the Army without keeping his wits about him, cast a quick glance down the table at his daughter and her fiancé before murmuring, 'It certainly sounds interesting.'

'Unfortunately, there are one or two problems...' Dominic began, before Helen gave a high, tinkling laugh.

'There certainly are!' she exclaimed, with a delicate shrug of her shoulders. 'Really, Daddy, the whole idea is simply absurd. Dominic is going to be abroad, and I can't possibly take leave from my job in the bank—not for something as silly as a mock battle. Besides, poor Laura simply couldn't cope with all the necessary organisation.'

'I'm sure I could manage,' Kate's aunt protested breathlessly. 'Martin and Alice...so helpful...such an interesting idea...' Her voice died away as Helen gave a determined shake of her head.

'No, it would be far too exhausting.' She gave the older woman a sweet, sympathetic smile. 'As I pointed out to Dominic, we couldn't allow you to take on such a burden.'

'Well, I think that's a load of rubbish!' Martin retorted. 'Putting on a mock Civil War battle would make a super day out for a lot of people...'

'But what about the damage they'd do to the lawns?' Helen interjected swiftly. 'And all the mess they'd leave behind them?'

'Nobody in this family is going to mind a bit of hard work clearing up after the battle,' Martin told her, a challenging note in his voice as he looked defiantly around the table.

'OK, Martin, I think we've got the message,' Dominic told him drily. 'However, Helen has made some very valid points, and...'

'Yes, we *all* know what Helen thinks!' Martin ground out savagely.

'Hey, hold it just a minute!' Kate exclaimed as Dominic's dark brows drew sharply together in an angry frown.

Goodness knows, she didn't want another row with Dominic, especially during her first meal here at the Priory, but she couldn't help feeling that her sympathies were heavily loaded on the side of her aunt and cousins.

'I may be wrong,' she continued as the table fell silent, 'but it doesn't sound as if any of you guys have ever taken part in these kind of mock battles before. And if you haven't, I can tell you that it's a whole lot of fun.'

'Do you have the same sort of thing in Canada?' Alice asked excitedly.

'Well, I'm not entirely sure. But my friend Jayne and I went to stay one summer with an old school friend who'd moved away to live down in Galveston, in Texas. Her parents were heavily into *The Lone Star*, outdoor drama production, and we sort of got involved with it too. It was really great!' Kate enthused, beaming happily around the table.

Helen gave another of her chilly, tinkling laughs, which Kate was beginning to find extremely irritating. 'I think you must be a little confused. We aren't talking about playing Cowboys and Indians, you know?'

'Neither am I,' Kate retorted crisply, refusing to be intimidated by Dominic's snotty English fiancée. 'The production was based on the founding of the Texas Republic. There was a cast of over eighty people—and lots of horses, cannon and gunfire;

they erected a huge house designed to be burnt to the ground, and there were some really fantastic battle scenes. You'd have loved it,' she told Martin with a smile.

'I wish I'd been there,' he said enviously.

'*And* we had people impersonating the Alamo heroes, Davy Crockett and Jim Bowie—together with Sam Houston and the Mexican general, Santa Ana. I can tell you it was a real gas! And since I was lucky enough to be allowed to help out behind the scenes, I reckon I had one of the greatest times of my life!'

'It sounds marvellous,' the general agreed.

'Yes, well,' Helen drawled silkily, 'I'm sure that's all very interesting. Of course, we can't expect *you* to understand our customs and traditions, here in England, but I don't think that what goes on in North America is likely to be of *any* interest to people over here,' she added scornfully.

Taken aback for a moment, Kate could feel a tide of crimson flooding across her face at Helen's heavily condescending, snide tone of voice. She was just trying to pull herself together when Dominic came unexpectedly to her rescue.

'There's very little difference between life in England and America nowadays,' he told his fiancée blandly. 'Or between America and Canada, for that matter. Even if—as Kate pointed out to me, some three months ago—they are "two very different nations",' he added, turning his head to grin down the table at the Canadian girl.

She gazed back at him in astonishment. What on earth had prompted Dominic to come so unexpectedly to her support? Wow, wonders would never cease! However, it looked as if he'd better watch out, because although everyone else around the table seemed to have missed his reference to their previous meeting in London, his fiancée certainly hadn't! Kate flinched as she saw that Helen was now staring at her with a fixed, angry gleam in her dark eyes.

Deciding that it might be a good idea to try and keep a low profile for a while, Kate allowed herself to be monopolised by George Wakeham for the rest of the meal. And afterwards, when coffee and liqueurs were served in the drawing-room, she adroitly managed to avoid both Dominic and his fiancée by prompting General Palmer to tell her all about his career in the Army.

However, after the guests had left and her young cousins had gone upstairs to bed, Kate found herself once again in the firing line.

She was just saying goodnight to Aunt Laura, and congratulating herself on getting through the evening unscathed, when Dominic announced that he wished to have a few brief words with her in his study.

Kate's heart sank. She had no idea what Dominic wanted to talk about—but it wasn't likely to be a quiet social conversation, was it? The thought of having yet another argument with him was distinctly unnerving.

'Er... well, I am rather tired...' she muttered uneasily.

'Of course she is,' Helen said firmly. 'Really, darling, you must be sensible. It's very late. Surely you can talk to that girl tomorrow?' she added, coming over to put a possessive hand on her fiancé's arm.

Kate gritted her teeth with annoyance at being referred to as 'that girl'. Helen might be going to marry Dominic, but that didn't give her the right to push other people around, did it?

'I won't keep Kate very long,' Dominic told his fiancée. And although his voice was even, containing no impatience or threat, there was something about the sheer force emanating from his still figure which seemed to disturb Helen's cool poise.

'I can't see why...' she flustered. 'I really do think...'

'*I* think it's been a long day, Helen. I'm sure that, like Kate, you're feeling tired,' he drawled smoothly.

'No, of course I'm not!' she snapped.

'Nevertheless, I intend to have a few private words with my stepmother's niece,' he replied blandly. 'So I suggest you go to bed—and I'll look forward to seeing you in the morning, hmm?'

After a swift glance at the tight, increasingly grim expression on Helen's face, Kate decided to fade from the scene as quickly as possible. The very last thing she needed was to find herself involved in a quarrel between these two arrogant, high-powered people. And, quite apart from anything else, she couldn't help being sorry for anyone about to get into a knock-out, drag-out fight with Dominic.

However, any feelings of sympathy or female solidarity were abruptly shattered as Helen gave a shrill, scornful laugh.

'I don't expect to be ordered upstairs to my room like a child!' she exclaimed angrily. 'And while I've nothing particularly against Kate—although she does seem to be displaying a quite *disgusting* amount of flesh—I'm quite sure she has better things to do than——'

'Oh, no, I haven't!' Kate declared, deciding she'd had quite enough of Helen for one evening. Giving Dominic a dazzling smile, which she hoped the other girl would mistake for one full of devastating sexual promise, she added huskily, 'In fact, I just can't *wait* to have some . . . er . . . private words with my *dear* cousin Dominic!'

CHAPTER FOUR

'THAT was a quite disgraceful performance!' Dominic told her grimly as he closed the study door behind them.

Kate didn't pretend to misunderstand him. 'Yes, I'm afraid you're right,' she agreed with a rueful sigh.

Sinking down into an armchair, she gazed about the study, which was decorated in sombre masculine colours of dark red and brown. It seemed a room particularly suited to its owner, she thought, watching apprehensively as Dominic took his place behind a heavy, red-leather-topped mahogany desk.

She was already deeply regretting her momentary mad impulse to cause the maximum amount of annoyance to Helen. Unfortunately, it looked as if she'd succeeded only too well! Remembering how the other girl had practically trembled with rage, before pulling herself together and icily promising Dominic that they would have 'a long, *serious* talk in the morning', Kate didn't doubt that he had an uncomfortable time ahead of him.

Although, now she came to think about it, her own immediate future in this house didn't look too rosy either. As far as she could see, Helen definitely wasn't the sort of person who was likely to either forgive or forget. Dominic himself had already made it perfectly clear that he wanted his new stepcousin to leave the house. So, now that his fiancée was likely to be breathing hell fire and brimstone as well...? Perhaps it *was* time she called it a day at Thornton Priory, and took off for pastures new?

Preoccupied with mentally packing her bags, and wondering if maybe a visit to Scotland might not be a good idea, Kate was interrupted by the sound of Dominic clearing his throat.

'I expect you've realised why I wanted to have a word with you,' he said.

'No, I'm afraid I haven't the faintest idea.' She shrugged her shoulders. 'Although, if I've upset Helen, I suppose I ought to say I'm sorry.'

'You don't sound at all sorry,' he told her sternly, his lips tightening with annoyance as she gazed back at him in stubborn silence.

Well, what did he expect—sackcloth and ashes? Kate asked herself sourly. It must be as clear as daylight that she and Helen hadn't taken to one another—so why should she try and pretend otherwise? Especially when the other girl had been so damned insulting! In fact, if anyone ought to be given an apology, it was probably herself. And there was no point in Dominic glaring at her with those icy-cold eyes of his. If he thought she was going to sit here meekly listening to a lecture, then he'd got another think coming!

'Well...?'

'I've said I'm sorry—and I don't see what more I can do,' she muttered. 'After all, I didn't ask to get dragged into a private fight between you and your girlfriend, did I? And I can't see any reason for her to make those catty remarks about either my nationality or my clothing,' she added in an aggrieved voice.

Dominic sighed and leaned back in his chair, his tanned face further darkened by the shadows thrown from the low reading lamp on his desk.

'Yes. Possibly Helen could have ... er ... chosen her words more carefully,' he conceded.

'You're so right!' Kate snapped. And then, to her complete surprise, she found herself asking, 'Are you *quite* certain that Helen is the right girl for you?'

Even as she heard herself saying the words, Kate realised she should have kept her mouth shut. She ought to know that Dominic was not the sort of guy to put up with any criticism of either himself or his fiancée.

She was quite correct—he wasn't.

'May I suggest that you mind your own business?' he retorted curtly.

'Ouch!' she muttered, wincing as he glared at her across the desk. 'I guess I was out of line there, right?'

'Right!' he echoed grimly. 'Quite frankly, I've come to the conclusion that you are without doubt the most persistently annoying girl I have *ever* come across. Not content with damaging my car, and causing me the maximum amount of embarrassment in London, you then turn up here, in Norfolk, marching into this house without an invitation ...'

'I *was* invited!'

' ... And within only a few hours, you're championing my brother's mad scheme; causing friction at the dinner table; asking extremely impertinent questions; and generally creating mayhem.'

'Me . . .? Creating mayhem?' She blinked at him in astonishment.

'Oh, yes—"mayhem" is definitely the word that comes to mind whenever I think about you, Kate!' he told her firmly, rising to his feet and glaring down at her for a moment, before walking over to a walnut veneered cabinet set in the far corner of the room.

'Of course, I can think of some other words which would do just as well,' he continued, with a harsh bark of sardonic laughter. 'Words such as "chaos", "commotion", "havoc" and "trouble" are a few that immediately come to mind. And, with further time for thought, I can probably come up with considerably more!' he added, opening the cabinet to reveal shelves of glasses and some heavy crystal decanters.

'All right, there's no need to be so nasty. I get the message,' Kate muttered glumly, before taking a deep breath. 'Look, I do realise that I was speaking out of turn just now.'

'That's putting it mildly,' he drawled coldly.

Kate scowled across the room at the loathsome man. 'I was only trying to say I'm sorry. I guess it isn't any business of mine who you're going to marry.'

'You're quite right, it isn't.'

'Oh, for heaven's sake! Why don't you just keep quiet for a moment and let me get this apology out of the way?' she ground out with exasperation.

Dominic gave a snort of harsh laughter as he removed the stopper from one of the crystal decanters. 'I'll say this for you, Kate, you're absolutely priceless!'

The hard note of sarcasm in his voice made her hackles rise. But she was amazed—and considerably annoyed—to see his shoulders shaking with amusement. Dominic might be able to find some humour in the situation, but she certainly didn't. In fact, she was fed up with always arguing with this man, and she had to admit that he was absolutely right: why should she care *who* he married? It didn't matter to her one way or another—right?

Kate frowned over at his tall, lithe figure as he closed the doors of the cabinet and moved slowly back towards the large mahogany desk.

So OK, he certainly wasn't the 'Hunk of the Month' as far as she was concerned. But, with his black hair liberally streaked with silver, and those startling blue eyes, she couldn't deny that Dominic was extremely handsome. In fact, seeing him clothed in the elegant black dinner-suit, which seemed designed to emphasise his broad shoulders and the sleek lines of his male body, she was surprised to find herself thinking that he looked very attractive—if not downright sexy!

To her utter dismay, Kate suddenly felt her mouth go dry, her hands becoming hot and clammy. What on earth was she doing, thinking about Dominic like this...? Oh, lord, she must be losing her marbles!

'There really doesn't seem to be much point in my staying here any longer...' she muttered nervously as she began to rise from her seat.

'Nonsense. Sit down, Kate,' he said firmly, his gaze narrowing as he looked down at the girl's flushed cheeks. 'There's absolutely no point in our quarrelling with one another,' he added, placing a glass on the table in front of her. 'Besides, it's getting late and I still haven't managed to discuss the business of this Civil War battle with you.'

'The battle?' She gave him a puzzled frown as she sank back down into her chair. 'You didn't say anything about wanting to talk to me about that.'

'You haven't given me a chance to do so,' he remarked flatly. 'So why don't you stop arguing with me, drink up your whisky, and allow me to explain the problem?'

'I don't want your rotten drink,' she grumbled, before catching his eye and giving him a slight, shamefaced grin. 'OK, you're quite right,' she admitted. 'I guess it's pointless for us to keep on quarrelling, and I'll freely admit that I shouldn't have got involved in other people's business.'

Dominic gave a dry rumble of sardonic laughter. 'No, you shouldn't. Although alas, I feel quite sure you always will!' he added, before taking a brief sip from his own glass. 'Frankly, Kate, I'm amazed that someone hasn't murdered you long before now!'

'Ha, ha,' she ground out bitterly. 'I thought you said you didn't want any more arguments?'

Dominic sighed, pushing a hand roughly through his thick dark hair. 'You're quite right—I don't. And why you and I should be constantly at one another's throats, I have no idea. Maybe we ought to try to turn back the clock? To forget what's happened in the past, and get to know one another properly, hmm?'

'That seems a bit of a tall order. Although I suppose I'm game if you are.' She gave him a cautious smile. 'But I thought you wanted to talk about the Civil War battle?'

'Yes, I'll come to that in a moment,' he said, leaning comfortably back in his chair. 'However, if we're going to become properly acquainted, I think you ought to tell me something about your life in Canada. Incidentally, I was very sorry to hear about your father's death,' he added quietly. 'Laura tells me he was a charming man.'

'Yes, Dad could always charm the birds from the trees,' Kate smiled ruefully. 'In fact, I guess he was just about the most charming, amusing man you could ever hope to meet. Unfortunately...' She hesitated for a moment, before explaining how her father had spent most of his life chasing one get-rich-quick scheme after another. None of his projects had ever really worked, and so it was fortunate that he had been unable to sell the farm.

'My mother died when I was only three years old, and since the land had originally belonged to her family she left it to me in some sort of complicated trust,' she told him. 'However, when Dad died and I found out just how much money he owed everyone...' She gave another shrug of her shoulders. 'Well, the only way to raise that sort of sum was to sell the farm.'

'I too lost my mother when I was young. So I know that life can't have been very easy for you,' Dominic said with a warm, sympathetic smile. 'I was, of course, very lucky to have Laura as my stepmother—even if I didn't always appreciate her at the time. But it's not the same as being cared for by one's own flesh and blood, is it?'

Kate was amazed to find Dominic so kind and understanding. 'Unfortunately, Dad never married again. I often used to wish he would,' she added wistfully. 'It would be fun to have some brothers and sisters—like Martin and Alice.'

He laughed. 'It's not so much fun when you have to play the part of a heavy older brother, I'm afraid. However, I think we're getting off the point. You still haven't told me about your farm.'

Under Dominic's skilful questioning, she found herself telling him all about her life to date. How, having only worked on the land, she felt extremely ill-equipped to earn a living in any other way; and about her subsequent decision to travel around Europe, before settling down to train for some profession.

'Hey, I bet you're a whizz in court,' she said suddenly, frowning bemusedly at him across the desk. 'I honestly don't know how you've done it,' she added darkly, 'but you seem to have got my whole life story from me—in five seconds flat!'

Dominic leaned back in his chair, his lips twitching with amusement. 'I'm not sure about being "a whizz"—but cross-examination of people is, after all, part of my job,' he reminded her blandly. 'However, we don't seem to have touched on the subject of your recent romance, do we?'

'I don't know what you're talking about,' she muttered, bitterly aware of the deep tide of colour rising up over her cheeks. Her brief, mad infatuation with Charles was a deeply embarrassing, hurtful episode which, even after three months, she could hardly bear to think about.

'But I understood that the destruction of my car was solely due to a lovers' tiff? Are you still involved with your...er...boyfriend?'

'Why don't *you* mind your own business?' she snapped.

'*Touché*, Kate!' he laughed ruefully, holding up his hands in mock surrender. 'However, I am glad you've been able to solve the small problem which has been troubling me over the past three months,' he continued. 'I couldn't understand how a young girl with no visible means of support could manage to pay my insurance company for the loss of my car.' He gave her a brief, sympathetic smile. 'I now see that it must have come from the proceeds of your farm sale. I'm sorry if it left you in any financial difficulty,' he added with concern.

'Well, I'm not exactly on the poverty line,' Kate assured him, surprised and unexpectedly touched by the note of warmth and kindness in his voice. 'However, since I did set myself a strict budget for this European trip, it looks as if I'm going to have to find a job, to pay for my plane fare back to Canada.'

'Ah, that's one of the items I wanted to talk to you about.'

'Yes, I thought it might be,' she remarked drily. 'Is this the point where you offer me that ticket for a coach trip around the British Isles?'

A faint flush covered his cheeks. 'No, of course not!' he snapped.

'But I thought you said...'

'You know very well—you wretched girl!—that you deliberately goaded me into making that threat this afternoon,' Dominic ground out with exasperation. 'In fact, I was just about to ask you to stay on here, at the Priory, for at least the next three weeks.'

Kate gazed at him in open-mouthed astonishment for a moment. 'Oh, boy, you've changed your tune, haven't you? I thought you couldn't stand me at any price?'

'No, that's not true,' he told her firmly. 'I'll agree that I was extremely annoyed about my car...'

'Annoyed?' She gave a hoot of laughter. 'Who are you kidding? You went completely bananas!'

Dominic sighed. 'You may be right,' he conceded. 'However, despite the fact that you've burst into my life like a whirling dervish, I'm quite prepared to admit that I find you a very interesting and...er...attractive girl.'

Kate's cheeks flushed, and she was astounded to find herself feeling ridiculously pleased for a few moments, before pulling herself sharply together. She'd better watch out—because this man was clearly as artful as a cage full of monkeys.

'You really want me to stay on here at the Priory?' she asked, and when he nodded she added bluntly, 'So what's the catch?'

'Catch?' He raised a dark, quizzical eyebrow.

'Come off it, Dominic!' she retorted, her suspicions confirmed as she caught the glint of laughter in his blue eyes.

He laughed, and shook his head in mock sorrow. 'How sad to find such cynicism—and in one so young!'

'Yeah—yeah,' she snorted with derision. 'Come on, spill the beans!'

'Well...' he hesitated for a moment, 'as you heard at dinner tonight, we do have some problems over this Civil War battle. I realise that Martin is desperately keen to have the show put on here. And, while he may regard me as an ogre at times, I'm very fond of the boy and I don't want to have to disappoint him. However, Helen does have a valid point. Laura's a dear woman, but even I have to admit that she's hopelessly impractical. Both Martin and Alice are too young to cope with everything, and Osborne is clearly too old. So, without someone to co-ordinate all the arrangements, it simply isn't a practical idea.'

'But surely you...'

Dominic shook his head. 'No, that's the whole point—I can't guarantee to be here. I'm due to act in a law case in Hong Kong,' he explained. 'Although the trial has been delayed, I could get a phone call to say it's on again any day now. And, unless there's someone to oversee all the arrangements, the whole battle affair could turn out to be a complete shambles.'

Kate nodded slowly. 'I suppose you're right,' she agreed reluctantly. 'Although it does seem a crying shame not to be able to put the battle on here.'

'I agree. Which is why I'm asking you to stay on here with us for a few more weeks.'

'You mean... You mean you want *me* to...um...'

'Yes,' he nodded. 'From what you told us all at dinner, you seem to have had some experience behind the scenes with these sort of mock battles. So do you think you would be able to co-ordinate all the arrangements? To act as a general dogsbody, and see that things don't get out of hand?'

'Well...yes, I suppose I could,' she murmured with a slight frown. 'But I don't see how I can help you out. I really do have to get a job, and...'

'I'm proposing that you should help me with the arrangements, and in return I'll pay for your flight back to Canada. What do you think about my suggestion?'

'What do I think...?' Kate gazed at him blankly for a moment. 'I think...' her voice rose indignantly '...in fact, I'm damn sure, that what you're suggesting is some kind of blackmail!'

Dominic grinned. 'Oh, no, my dear Kate. As you yourself pointed out to me earlier this afternoon, I'm the expert "legal eagle" around here,' he drawled mockingly. 'I can assure you that my proposal is merely a sensible arrangement between the two of us.'

Kate glared at him with deep resentment for a moment, but she couldn't see any way out of the impasse—not if Martin was to have the Civil War battle he'd set his heart on. And there was also the business of her flight ticket back to Canada.

'OK, it seems that you've got me over a barrel,' she sighed helplessly. 'I guess I'll be staying on here to help out with the arrangements for the show.'

'I hoped you would,' Dominic murmured blandly, his eyes gleaming with sardonic amusement.

'However, I'd better give you fair warning that I haven't had a lot of experience,' she told him firmly. 'There's no way I can pretend to be an expert on these sort of shows. So I hope you haven't got the wrong idea?'

He shook his dark head. 'The chances are that I'm going to be here. And even if I'm not, we'll probably have covered most of the ground work before I have to go to Hong Kong,' he assured her, before raising his glass. 'I think we should drink a toast to our future...er...co-operation, don't you?'

Determined not to rise to the horrid man's bait— he was clearly just trying to rub salt in her wounds— Kate took a cautious sip from her glass. 'Mmm, this isn't at all bad. What is it?'

'It's a very fine, pure malt whisky from a small Highland distillery in the north of Scotland. So kindly treat it with respect, and don't toss it down...'

'Agh...!' Kate choked, clutching her throat and going puce in the face, tears streaming down her cheeks.

'I said *don't* toss it down your throat like Coca-Cola!' Dominic ground out with exasperation, going quickly to her aid as she jumped up from her chair, staggering about the room and gasping for breath.

'W-wow! That s-stuff really...really p-packs a p-punch!' she wheezed and stuttered, before Dominic caught hold of her, quickly slapping her on the back.

'What an idiot you are!' he told her sternly, taking out his handkerchief to wipe the tears from her eyes.

Kate could only nod in agreement, leaning weakly against his broad shoulder for a moment, until the fall-out from the atomic bomb in her stomach had begun to subside.

'I guess it wasn't too...too c-clever. But the truth is, I don't normally drink much alcohol. Which is probably just as well,' she added with a nervous laugh. 'Because it's left me feeling...well, a bit as though I've suddenly lost my balance.'

Dominic muttered something under his breath. She thought it sounded like, 'You're not the only one.' But he seemed perfectly steady on his feet, she thought as she vowed to herself that she would never touch that sort of firewater ever again. There was no doubt about it: the Scots must have stomachs lined with asbestos!

'How are you feeling now?' he enquired. It was the oddly constrained, tense note in his voice which caused her to raise her head and gaze up into his blue eyes.

It must be the whisky whizzing through her body that was making her feel so peculiar, she thought distractedly as her heart suddenly began thumping fiercely like a heavy sledgehammer out of control. And it was just as well that she didn't normally drink strong liquor, because that wasn't the only weird effect it appeared to be having. The room seemed to be shrinking about them—a dark mist swirling about their two still figures as her eyes remained firmly locked by the intense, searching, almost hypnotic gaze with which he seemed to be invading her very soul.

The silence lengthened, the tension mounting, second by second, until Kate could feel it almost pounding against her skull.

How long they stood staring silently at one another, she had no idea. The strange spell was only broken by the harsh, muffled sound of Dominic swearing violently under his breath, before she found herself being quickly picked up and then dumped unceremoniously down on a nearby couch.

'Hey, what do you think you're doing?' she demanded, struggling to sit up among the soft cushions.

'Keeping myself well out of the way of temptation!' he told her grimly.

'Temptation?' She gazed at him with bewilderment. 'What on earth are you talking about?'

'Kindly pull your dress down,' he continued, ignoring her question. 'And while I'm on the subject, I hope that tomorrow night you'll find some garment more suitable to wear than that apology for a dress,' he added in a stern, hard voice.

'OK, I know it's not brilliant,' she retorted angrily. 'But it's all I had to wear. I didn't know you were going to give a hoity-toity dinner party, did I? But if it makes you feel any better, I'm intending to buy myself something else to wear tomorrow. Satisfied?'

He gave a harsh snort of mirthless laughter. 'No, of course I'm not satisfied, but at least we'll be able to ask George Wakeham to the house again. He's obviously not used to meeting half-nude women. The poor chap was thoroughly embarrassed.'

'How dare you?' Kate gasped, sitting bolt upright on the couch. 'And I wouldn't feel too sorry for your friend George Wakeham if I were you,' she added bitterly. 'He wasn't embarrassed—he was

just being damned lecherous. Which, as far as I'm concerned, is only one degree worse than being a prudish old maid like yourself!'

'Oh, really?' Dominic drawled in a silky, menacing tone.

'Yes, *really*!' Kate glared up at him, suddenly swept by an almost overwhelming, irresistible urge to hurt this supercilious man, to puncture his extraordinary self-possession. How dared he stand there, looking down his superior nose at her, as if she were some strange, weird creature from another planet?

'Not only are you thoroughly nasty—and incidentally, *don't* think I've forgotten how you callously dumped me in that London police station, because I certainly haven't! But as far as I can see, you're also the perfect partner for that awful girl Helen. She thought I looked "disgusting" too, didn't she?' Kate raged. 'So I guess you two really deserve each other! And, while I'm on the subject...'

'Kindly keep your voice down!' he grated as her boiling anger and fury reverberated around the room.

'No, why should I?' she yelled loudly. 'It's about time someone told you a few home truths. You toffee-nosed, arrogant man—it's abundantly clear that you've got nothing but icy-cold water in your veins,' she added with a high-pitched malicious laugh. 'Frankly, *dear* Dominic, I don't reckon you're made of flesh and blood like the rest of us. As far as I can see, you're nothing but a...a cardboard cut-out!'

As her father had frequently pointed out in the past, Kate had an unfortunate tendency to ignore the safe, sensible path in life; often apt to forget that discretion is generally the better part of valour. And, as she later acknowledged privately to herself, losing her temper with Dominic had proved to be a very grave mistake!

One minute she was sitting bolt upright on the couch, giving him a piece of her mind, and then, a second later, she found her arm grabbed as Dominic jerked her off the couch . . . and into his arms.

'A cardboard cut-out, am I?' he roared savagely, his arms tightening around her like bands of steel.

'Leave me alone, you dreadful man!' she screeched, suddenly frightened by the cold fury in his stormy blue eyes, and realising—when it was too late—that this was one time when she had definitely Gone Too Far.

'Not made of flesh and blood . . . ?' he hissed menacingly through clenched teeth.

'OK, I was wrong. I'm sorry. You're terrific . . . a wonderful personality . . . really fantastic!' she gabbled helplessly. 'No—*no*!'

Kate's gasp was stifled by the swift descent of his dark head, his mouth closing over hers and ruthlessly crushing her lips in a heartless, punishing kiss. Trying to wriggle out of his arms, or even to move her head away, proved fruitless, and she became breathless beneath the force of his lips and her own exertion as she beat her fists against his broad shoulders, in a completely vain attempt to escape.

And then... well, she was so preoccupied with putting up a strong resistance that it was some moments before she realised that his arms had loosened slightly, and that he wasn't kissing her quite so fiercely. In fact, the mouth possessing hers was now moving softly and sensuously over her lips, evoking a trembling response which she was finding almost impossible to resist. So impossible, indeed, that when he slowly lifted his head, gazing down at her with a strained, taut expression on his face, she could only stare blindly back at him in dazed confusion.

'How... er... how quite extraordinary!' he murmured, taking a deep breath and closing his eyes for a moment. 'I wonder—just as an experiment, of course—would you... er... mind if I kissed you again?'

'You want to kiss me—*again*...? Kate gasped incredulously, as her arms crept up to wind themselves tightly about his neck. 'Of course you can't! I've never heard anything quite so—so ridiculous!' she protested weakly, unconsciously pressing herself closer to his firm body, a deep knot of tremulous desire flaring into life as he lowered his head once more, his mouth moving softly and tantalisingly over the outline of her trembling lips.

'Quite... quite ridiculous!' he breathed huskily as her lips parted involuntarily under the delicate pressure, allowing him to slowly and erotically savour the soft moistness within.

It was as if a stream of fire was scorching through her veins beneath his deepening kiss, her body becoming soft and yielding as he moulded it tightly to his own. She was aware of nothing but the wild passion which held her in thrall; trembling at the erotic excitement at Dominic's own obvious arousal, the sensual touch of his hand moving slowly down her back as he unzipped her dress, edging it down over her shoulders.

'My God, what's happening to us ... ?' he whispered huskily, trailing his lips down the curve of her neck towards the warm, burgeoning fullness of her firm breasts—when the silence of the room was suddenly shattered.

'Stand still and don't move—we've got you covered!' a voice called out as, with a loud crash, the study door was thrown violently open.

CHAPTER FIVE

AFTER a disturbed night, tossing and turning in a state of perpetual motion, Kate woke up the next morning feeling sluggish and heavily depressed. Putting out a hand to her bedside table, she was horrified to note the time on her small travelling clock.

Half past ten! How *could* she have overslept like that? And bang goes the idea of escaping from Thornton Priory at the first light of dawn, she thought wearily. There was no way that she could now hope to creep silently out of the house. At this time of day, and with so many people around, she was bound to be spotted.

Lying back on the pillows, Kate stared up at the top of her four-poster bed, unable to prevent the memories of last night's fiasco from stealing insidiously into her mind. A brilliant tide of colour swept across her pale cheeks as she recollected, with hideous clarity, that final scene in the study. It had been running through her brain all night, jerkily frame by frame, like one of those old silent movies.

She knew she would never forget the sight of Aunt Laura, timidly brandishing a steel poker; nor the dressing-gowned figure of Martin, holding what looked remarkably like an ancient blunderbuss in one hand, with his other arm thrown protectively around Alice.

Kate's first startled yelp of shock and dismay had been abruptly cut short as Dominic, quickly moving to shield her from the intruders' gaze, had swiftly zipped up her dress before turning back to face his family.

'We thought we heard burglars!'

'I wasn't feeling at all brave, but Martin said...'

'Such a noise...loud voices...so frightened!'

'For goodness' sake, will you all please *shut up*!' Dominic bellowed angrily over the noisy babble as Martin, Alice and Aunt Laura all spoke loudly at once.

'Are you sure there isn't a burglar in here?' Alice's voice broke into the sudden silence. 'Martin said there was a terrific noise, and...'

'I've never heard such nonsense!' Dominic retorted in crushing tones, before turning his icy-cold eyes on Martin. 'And what, may I ask, do you think you're doing with that antique monstrosity? It certainly hasn't been fired for the past two hundred years. So kindly put it back over the fireplace in the hall where it belongs.'

Martin gave his older half-brother a sheepish grin as he lowered the ancient weapon.

'I know I must look a bit daft, but Ma had already grabbed the poker, and it was all I could find in a hurry. There's no need for you to laugh,' he added belligerently as Dominic gave a contemptuous snort of derision. 'I mean, a lot of burglars carry weapons these days, don't they?'

'But—but there doesn't seem to have been a burglar,' Aunt Laura pointed out breathlessly. 'I don't...I simply don't understand what's been going on in here,' she added plaintively.

Kate, who was sheltering behind Dominic's tall figure, and frantically endeavouring to do something about her dishevelled appearance, quickly realised that it was a complete waste of time. Her aunt might be a little confused, but after one quick glance over Dominic's shoulder at the faces of her two young cousins, it was only too clear that they must have a pretty good idea of what had been 'going on' in the study!

Now, as she looked back on the disastrous episode, Kate could see that it was at this point that she had, unfortunately, completely lost her head.

Instead of being sensible and trying to bluff her way out of the situation, she had abandoned any attempt at poise or sophistication by making a cowardly, chicken-hearted dash across the room. Intent on fleeing upstairs to her bedroom, she was foiled at the last moment in her bid to escape—by the sudden appearance of Helen.

Standing framed in the doorway, looking cool and remarkably soignée in a black lace negligé, Helen raised a scornful eyebrow as she gazed at Kate's bedraggled appearance.

'Well, really!' she drawled. 'What *have* you been doing with yourself? And why are you still down here, causing all this commotion? Surely you should have been upstairs and in bed long ago?' she added, her voice sharpening as she gazed past the distraught Canadian girl towards the other figures standing motionless in the study.

The whole situation was proving far too much for Kate to cope with. 'You're right, it is late. I'm just . . . er . . . just going upstairs,' she gabbled nervously, trying to inch her way past Helen's rigid figure.

'I don't understand...'

'Neither do I—so why don't you ask *him*?' Kate cried wildly, spinelessly throwing Dominic to the wolves as she barged her way past his fiancée and out into the hall.

As she bolted up the staircase to take refuge in her bedroom, her final impression of the scene downstairs had been Helen's cold, clear voice demanding that Dominic give her an *immediate* explanation of what had been going on in the study.

So what on earth was she going to do now? Kate asked herself, giving a heavy sigh as she pushed a distraught hand through her tousled hair. Unfortunately, there didn't seem to be much she could do—other than to apologise to both her aunt and cousins, before leaving Thornton Priory as quickly as possible.

Her visit had clearly been doomed from the start. In fact, when she had arrived and discovered that Dominic was not in Hong Kong, she ought to have jumped on to her motorcycle and high-tailed it straight back to London. That was what any sensible person would have done. Right?

But not Kate Macaulay. Oh, no, *you* weren't going to let yourself be pushed around. And just look where it's got you! Kate told herself in disgust. Nor was there much consolation to be found in the fact that Dominic himself was also likely to be in hot water. Not when it meant losing the only family she had in the world—just as she was getting to know them. I hope Helen gives him a really, *really* hard time, Kate thought viciously. Because if anyone richly deserved everything he'd got coming to him, it was Dominic Smith-Farrell. What a swine the man was!

Just look at the way he'd lost his temper, and pulled her into his arms, and then . . . Oh no! *No*—she was definitely *not* going to think about the extraordinary, mind-boggling sensations produced by the touch of his lips on hers.

Kate turned over, burying her flaming face in the pillows as she tried to close her mind and body to the embarrassing, shameful recollections of how she had moaned with pleasure in Dominic's arms. What on earth had come over her? she asked herself miserably.

It wasn't just the disgraceful fact that she had somehow become involved with a man who was engaged to another woman. Goodness knows, that was bad enough. But Kate totally failed to understand her own behaviour. She had had plenty of boyfriends in the past. However, none of them—not even Charles—had come anywhere near to provoking the confusion and turmoil she was feeling at this moment; the wild mixture of excitement and depression raging through her veins, or the deep throbbing ache in the pit of her stomach.

However, it was no good lying here hacking over the disastrous events of last night, Kate told herself glumly. She had absolutely no idea of what she was going to do, but she *must* try and come up with a constructive plan of action. And that was going to require a cup of strong coffee. Despite all the excellent advice nowadays from the health food lobby, she simply couldn't begin to function in the mornings without a hefty dose of caffeine. Unfortunately that would mean going downstairs into either the kitchen or the dining-room—*not* a very good idea in her present circumstances.

As she bit her lip with indecision, the problem was taken out of her hands by a knock on her door, quickly followed by the appearance of Aunt Laura carrying a tray.

'I'm sorry to be so late, dear. But the whole house is at sixes and sevens this morning,' the older woman said, walking over to place the breakfast tray down on a small stool at the end of the bed.

'A pot of coffee—how wonderful!' Kate groaned happily, before suddenly recalling the scene in the study last night. 'You really shouldn't have bothered. I . . . er . . . I'm ashamed to say I seem to have overslept,' she added, her cheeks burning with embarrassment.

'There's no need to worry about that, dear, especially as everyone else seems to have got up late this morning. And I can't tell you how pleased we all were to hear the good news!' Her aunt gave her a warm smile.

'The good news?' Kate echoed faintly.

'Dominic's told us how you've agreed to help him with all the organisation for the mock battle,' Aunt Laura beamed happily down at her niece. 'I'm so grateful, dear. As you can imagine, Martin is absolutely thrilled to bits!'

'Yes, well . . . um . . . I'll be happy to do anything I can.'

'And of course, once Dominic had explained everything, we all quite understood why there was so much noise in the study last night.'

Kate blinked nervously. 'You do . . . ?'

'It was really *very* naughty of Dominic to have given you such a large glass of neat whisky—especially if you aren't used to drinking strong alcohol. If you drank it all down in one gulp, it's no wonder you were shouting for help!'

As Kate gazed speechless up at her aunt, the older woman gave her a warm, sympathetic smile. 'I can promise you, dear, that both Helen and I were *very* cross with him for being so thoughtless. I do hope you're feeling better this morning?'

'Yes...er...I'm fine,' Kate muttered, finding her voice at last as Aunt Laura, with another murmured warning about the dangers of strong liquor, left the room.

With a deep groan, Kate threw herself back down on to the pillows. It was all so darned unfair! She, who had spent so many hours agonising about last night's fracas in the study, was now being labelled as an innocent drunkard, while that truly awful man Dominic Smith-Farrell had merely received a telling-off from his stepmother and fiancée. Whoever had said there was no justice in the world was absolutely right!

Half an hour later, after ignoring the food on her tray while she fortified herself with two steaming cups of hot coffee, Kate still hadn't decided what to do. She didn't want to disappoint Martin, of course, but it wasn't too late for her to cut and run back to London, where she was sure to be able to earn the money for her ticket home. So, if she *was* going to stay on here at the Priory, it all seemed to hinge on the relationship between Dominic and his fiancée.

There was no point in pretending that she and the English girl had taken to one another, because they clearly hadn't. However, her arrival here at the Priory hadn't started off on exactly the right foot, and the last thing Kate wanted was to cause any more trouble.

Of course, it wasn't the end of the world if a man, while engaged to one girl, had been discovered with his arms about another. And although she was furious with Dominic, she had to admit that he'd been pretty smart. While not exactly telling a lie—although he'd been darned economical with the truth!—he'd obviously kept his head, and managed to talk his way out of a very tight corner.

But the question still remained: did Helen really believe that Kate's dishevelled appearance had been caused by the demon drink—and the result of being slapped so vigorously on the back? Or did she have a good idea of what her fiancée had been doing with his arms around Kate?

And *I* wouldn't mind knowing what he thought he was doing either! Kate thought grimly, pacing up and down the bedroom. Not that she had any intention of asking him, of course. The very last thing she wanted was any further close involvement with the awful man. Goodness knows how it had happened—she didn't even *like* Dominic, for heaven's sake—but she couldn't deny that he seemed to be affecting her in a most peculiar manner.

'Pull yourself together!' she muttered angrily to herself, disgusted to note the way her hands were trembling as she poured another cup of coffee. 'If you're going to break out in a hot flush every time you think about the man, it looks like you're in serious trouble! In fact, the sooner you shake the dust of Thornton Priory off your feet, the better!'

'Do you always talk out loud to yourself?'

'Agh...!' Kate screeched, almost jumping out of her skin with shock as a voice spoke from behind her. 'Oh, goodness, I didn't hear you come in, Alice,' she gasped, grabbing some tissues and trying to mop up the coffee which she had spilled all over herself and the carpet.

'Oops—I'm sorry if I startled you,' said Alice, picking up the cup from the floor.

'You sure did. How about knocking on the door next time, huh?' Kate told her grumpily, dabbing at a coffee stain on her thin silk wrap.

Goodness knows what Alice thought she looked like. The long, shapeless black dress didn't do a thing for the girl. Besides which, the sight of her young face painted green on one side and red on another was enough to turn anyone's stomach! Why didn't her mother, or Dominic, do something about these ghastly outfits? If Alice was *her* sister, she'd have locked her in her bedroom and refused to let her out—not until the girl had changed her clothes, and scrubbed her face clean, Kate thought.

Alice ran into the bathroom, returning with a damp wash-cloth. 'Here,' she said, handing it to Kate. 'My mother says cold water's the only thing to get rid of coffee stains.'

'Thanks, kid—maybe you aren't all bad!' Kate told her, giving her a wry smile. She had recovered from the shock of Alice's sudden appearance, and it really wasn't fair to take out her own fraught mental state on the girl.

'I really just came in to say a big "thank you". It's really terrific news that you're going to stay and help us with the Civil War battle,' Alice said enthusiastically, sitting down on the bed and helping herself to some toast and marmalade.

It looked as if Alice had also swallowed her brother's story, Kate told herself, knowing she ought to be relieved that there wasn't going to be any fuss or scandal about the episode in the study last night. However, she couldn't help feeling extremely irritated and incensed at the way Dominic seemed to be getting away with murder.

'Well, I would like to help in putting on the show, but . . .'

'Martin's over the moon about it all, of course,' Alice continued blithely. 'In fact, he suggested that it might be a good idea for me to give you a tour of the house, and tell you all about our family history. Just to put you in the picture, if you see what I mean?'

Kate's heart sank. Thanks to that awful man Dominic, it now looked as though she was well and truly stuck. How could she possibly disappoint her cousins, who were obviously so excited about the forthcoming show?

'Yes . . . er . . . that was nice of Martin,' she agreed weakly.

'Not really,' Alice mumbled with her mouth full. 'Actually, I think he was simply trying to get me out of the dining-room. Old Dom always gets cross when he sees me dressed like this. . . .'

'I'm not surprised!'

'...And, since he came down to breakfast in a really *filthy* mood, it seemed quite a good idea to make myself scarce!'

'Hmm...yes, I can see it might,' Kate murmured, making a mental note to keep well out of Dominic's way, for as long as possible. 'Although, if he gets annoyed whenever he sees you in those awful clothes and make-up,' she continued, 'I can't say I'm too surprised. I hope you'll forgive me for saying so, but quite frankly, kid, you look absolutely revolting!'

'But that's the whole idea, you see?'

'No, I can't say I do,' Kate shrugged. 'I'm not suggesting that you have to wear a frilly dress—but what's wrong with a clean pair of jeans?'

Alice laughed. 'Nothing at all. But I had this super plan. You know how Helen always looks as if she's just stepped out of a fashion magazine?'

'I know what you mean,' Kate agreed with feeling.

'Well, I thought that if she always saw me wearing really disgusting clothes and make-up, she might go off the whole idea of marrying Dominic. What do you think? Quite honestly,' the girl added desperately, 'I'd do *anything* to save my brother from that *awful* woman!'

'Oh, Alice...!' Kate sighed, going over to the girl and putting an arm around her thin shoulders. 'It really isn't going to work, you know. And if your brother is in love with Helen, you really shouldn't try and interfere with their relationship,' she added softly.

'Yes, I know,' Alice sniffed. 'But she's going to make him *so* unhappy—— Oh, goodness—speak of the devil!' she gasped suddenly, quickly leaping to her feet and dashing across the room into the adjacent bathroom.

For a few seconds, Kate gazed in open-mouthed astonishment at the now firmly closed bathroom door. And then she too heard the sound of firm, steady footsteps approaching down the hall towards her bedroom; a noise which Alice's young ears had picked up far sooner than her own.

'May I come in?' asked Helen, barely bothering to knock as she coolly opened the door and entered the room.

Yes, 'cool' was the word for Helen, all right, Kate thought glumly, gazing at the other girl as she marched confidently across the carpet towards her.

Carrying a silver-mounted whip, and clearly about to go riding, Helen was immaculately dressed in slim cream-coloured jodhpurs and long, gleaming black boots, beneath a cream silk blouse, whose high round collar was pinned at the neck with a gold and diamond brooch. Unfortunately, while the English girl looked like a million dollars, Kate was only too well aware of her own bedraggled appearance in the thin dressing-gown, her long mane of hair still tangled and uncombed.

'Hi, Helen—what can I do for you?' she asked apprehensively, quickly turning away to pick up her brush and dragging it through her hair.

'Not a great deal, I imagine,' the other girl drawled coldly, wrinkling her nose as she gazed around the room. 'Do you always live in such chaos?' she asked, not bothering to disguise her scorn and contempt at the half-unpacked suitcase, the untidy piles of clothing and make-up.

'I only arrived here at the Priory yesterday afternoon,' Kate muttered, determined not to get into an argument with the other girl. 'I haven't really had much time to sort everything out.'

'I wouldn't be in too much of a hurry to unpack, if I were you,' Helen told her flatly. 'In fact, I've come in here to find out just when you're planning to go.'

'Go...?' Kate echoed, seemingly preoccupied with brushing her hair. 'Go where, exactly?'

'I really couldn't care less!' the other girl snapped. 'Just as long as you leave this house as soon as possible.'

Oh-oh! It looked as if Helen was about to lose her temper, Kate thought nervously. Glancing sideways through her eyelashes, she saw that the other girl was now tapping the whip angrily against her long, shiny black boots.

'I don't think I can leave just yet,' she said. 'I've promised Dominic that I'd stay and help him with the mock battle.'

'The idea of such a show is complete nonsense!' snapped Helen. 'Crowds of people, all treating this place like a football stadium. I shudder to think of the mess which will be left behind.' Helen's voice rose angrily. 'The house and grounds will be completely *ruined*!'

Kate shrugged. 'You may be right. But, since my aunt and cousins have decided to go ahead with the battle, there doesn't seem to be much point in bellyaching about it, does there?'

'You really don't care, do you?' the other girl demanded furiously. 'You turn up here, from the wilds of Canada, and promptly begin making as much trouble as possible!'

'Now, just a minute!' Kate snapped. 'You know darned well that whether this battle goes ahead or not has absolutely nothing to do with me.'

'Of course it has. The whole idea would have died a natural death, if you hadn't gone on and on at dinner last night, boring us all rigid about that stupid show in Texas,' Helen said bitterly. 'And now I hear that you've craftily wormed your way into running the show...'

'Oh, come on!' Kate protested, surprised to find the other girl so concerned about the mock battle. 'Dominic has asked me to assist him...'

'Yes, so I've heard!'

'...And in return he's giving me my plane fare back to Canada. It's just a business arrangement— right?'

Helen gave a high-pitched, shrill peal of laughter. 'Oh, is that what you call it? Maybe you can tell me exactly what "business" was going on last night?'

'I...er...I don't know what you mean,' Kate muttered, painfully aware of her cheeks flushing beneath the other girl's angry glare.

'Don't act the innocent with me!' Helen snarled. 'I want to know what you were doing with my fiancé in the study last night!'

Kate took a deep breath. 'I was doing absolutely nothing,' she lied firmly, wondering why she was bothering to try and save Dominic's skin, as she stared the other girl straight in the eye.

'I don't believe you!'

'Well, I can't help that.' Kate tried to give a nonchalant shrug. 'It's no secret that Dominic and I don't much like each other. In fact, I'm still cross with him for giving me that drink and letting me almost choke to death. He was merely hitting me on the back when everyone burst into the room,' she added, with as much conviction as she could manage.

'You're lying!' Helen snapped.

'Oh, for heaven's sake, why don't you cool it?' Kate retorted. 'I couldn't care less about Dominic. After all, he's engaged to you, isn't he? And since you're both obviously such cold-blooded fish, I really can't think of two people more suited to each other! Now,' she added, putting her hairbrush down on the dressing-table, '*if* you don't mind, I'd like to get dressed.'

For one awful moment, watching as the other girl's fingers tightened on the whip, Kate wondered if Helen was going to be tempted to use it. However, after a fierce internal struggle, she turned on her heel and stalked away across the room.

'You haven't managed to fool me, Miss Macaulay,' she snarled, opening the door. 'If you think I'm going to allow you to steal both this house *and* my fiancé from me, then you're very much mistaken!'

Sagging with relief as Helen slammed the door loudly behind her, Kate took a deep breath before going over to knock on the bathroom door.

'You can come out now, Alice,' she called, feeling as though she were in the middle of a French farce, with bedroom doors opening and closing every five seconds. 'How much of that did you hear?'

Alice shrugged. 'Not a lot, unfortunately,' she confessed, to Kate's relief. 'These old walls are so thick that it's practically impossible to hear what's going on on the other side. Was Horrid Helen in a frightful temper?'

'Mmm, yes, she was,' said Kate, surprised to find herself shaking from nervous tension.

'Well, I expect that's because old Dom and Helen had a huge row just before breakfast. That's one of the reasons why I left the dining-room as soon as possible. Honestly,' Alice confided with a happy grin, 'the atmosphere between them was so thick, you could practically cut it with a knife!'

Kate frowned, becoming guiltily aware that she ought not to be encouraging Alice to gossip about her brother's fiancée, or to call her names.

'Oh, come on, kid. Even if you don't like the woman, she is Dominic's choice,' she pointed out quietly.

'But that's the problem—none of us can understand *why*! I mean, he's got lots of money, and is very good-looking, isn't he?'

'Er...yes, I suppose so,' Kate muttered lamely.

'Well, he is terribly old, of course,' Alice conceded. 'But some of my school friends think he's quite attractive. Even Nancy Stevens, who's crazy about boys, told me she thinks he's dead sexy!' the girl added with a slightly embarrassed grin. 'So you see, there must be *lots* of women who'd like to marry him. Martin and I have been hoping and praying that Dom will ditch Horrid Helen and choose someone else—but she clings to him like a leech.'

'Now, Alice, you really mustn't...'

'But you don't understand just how important it is for Dominic to be happy,' the girl said earnestly. 'It's all because of his first fiancée, you see.'

Kate frowned in puzzlement. 'Dominic's first fiancée...?'

'I was too young to know much about it, and Dominic never mentions the subject, of course,' Alice confided. 'But my mother told me that she was a really super girl. Well, she went off to visit her father somewhere in Africa—and got bitten by the wrong sort of mosquito. It seems that she didn't take any anti-malaria pills, and unfortunately she died soon after getting back to this country.'

'That's terrible!' exclaimed Kate, surprised to find herself suddenly feeling desperately sorry for Dominic. 'Your brother must have been awfully unhappy.'

Alice nodded. 'My mother says he was absolutely devastated—and it's taken him years to get over it. And that's why we all want him to be happy, and marry the right person, now.'

Kate held her tightly for a moment, then said slowly, 'I know you mean well, sweetie. But I think you really must leave your brother to sort out his own affairs. Helen wouldn't be your or my choice, but she is Dominic's, isn't she? I'm sure that if he felt she wasn't right for him, he'd break it off like a shot. So,' she added bracingly, giving the girl some tissues, 'why don't you dry your eyes? And if you don't mind waiting for a few minutes while I have a quick shower and get dressed, I guess I'll take you up on that offer to show me around the house.'

After wrestling fairly successfully with the ancient plumbing, Kate emerged from the bathroom some minutes later busily drying her long, wet hair.

'Hey, Alice, I thought I might go shopping after lunch,' she muttered from beneath the large, bulky towel draped over her head. 'Do you know of any good local dress shops?'

She was shocked and startled to find her words greeted by a deep, sardonic laugh. 'I don't think Alice is going to be much help—not unless you want to look like Lady Macbeth!'

Kate gasped, throwing back the towel to discover that Alice had apparently—once again—disappeared into thin air. The room was now quite empty, apart from Dominic's tall figure leaning casually against one of the bedposts.

'For heaven's sake, this place is getting like Grand Central Station!' she grumbled, throwing the towel on to a nearby chair and nervously tightening the sash of her dressing-gown. 'What on earth are *you* doing here?'

He raised a dark eyebrow. 'How strange,' he drawled caustically. 'I was under the impression that this was my house.'

She flinched at the heavy note of sarcasm in his voice. 'But it's *my* bedroom while I'm staying in this house,' she retorted breathlessly, her cheeks flushing with embarrassment as she saw his clear blue eyes flicking dismissively over her damp, dishevelled figure.

It really wasn't her day, Kate told herself gloomily. She'd already had to put up with Helen, looking cool and immaculate as she'd stared contemptuously down her long nose—as if Kate was something nasty that the cat had dragged into the house. And now here was Dominic, looking equally smart and elegant in a short-sleeved black shirt tucked into a pair of close-fitting beige jodhpurs, his long legs encased in shiny black leather riding boots.

It simply wasn't fair—not when she herself was looking such a mess! Kate thought miserably, trying to ignore a most confusing sick fluttering feeling in the pit of her stomach. And, belatedly realising that she was stark naked beneath her thin silk gown, she quickly pulled the edges of the garment tighter about her.

'I did knock on the door.' Dominic shrugged his broad shoulders. 'However, since you were in the bathroom, you obviously didn't hear me.'

'OK, OK,' she muttered, putting up a trembling hand to brush the long wet tendrils of hair from her face. 'So what do you want?'

'I merely want to have a word with you.'

'As far as I'm concerned, we had plenty of words last night. And if that's your idea of conversation, I'm in no hurry to repeat the experience!' Kate told him bitterly.

Dominic stared across at her for a long moment, before giving a heavy sigh and walking over to gaze out of the window. 'That's precisely why I wanted to see you. I've told my family that we...that is, I...er...was entirely to blame,' he said with his back to her, continuing to stare out of the window. 'I shouldn't have given you such a strong drink, and...'

'Yeah, yeah.' Kate waved an impatient hand. 'I've already heard that story. And incidentally, thanks a bunch for telling everyone I was staggering around blind drunk!' she added grimly.

'I'm sorry about that, Kate,' he murmured, turning back to face her.

'I bet!' she ground out, her anger fuelled by the way he was staring at the thin silk garment clinging so tightly to the full generous curves of her damp body. 'How you expected them to believe that load of baloney beats me!'

'I can assure you that my explanation was accepted by all the family,' he said stiffly.

'Oh, yeah?' She gave a snort of harsh laughter. 'Well, I'll agree that you seem to have got away with it as far as Aunt Laura and Alice are concerned,' she admitted grudgingly. 'But I'm afraid you're out of luck with dear Helen. I've already had a visit from Miss Frigidaire this morning, and I can tell you that she doesn't believe one word of your rotten story!'

'Kindly leave Helen out of this discussion,' he grated, a muscle beating in his clenched jaw.

'I only wish I could!'

There was a long pause as they glared at one another, the silence eventually broken as Dominic gave a heavy sigh, roughly brushing a hand through his thick black hair.

'I do realise that you've been placed in a very awkward situation, Kate,' he said in a quiet voice. 'I'll try and do what I can to...er...sort matters out with my fiancée.'

'And the best of luck!' she snapped, before giving a heavy sigh and shrugging her shoulders. Quite honestly, it had already been quite an exhausting morning, and she was heartily sick and tired of always quarrelling with Dominic. 'Don't panic—you can relax,' she told him drily. 'When Helen came in here this morning, I supported your story. I'm not saying that the words didn't stick in my throat, because they did!—but I figured you were in quite enough trouble without my adding any more wood to the fire. Right?'

'Quite right,' he agreed with a grin, ruefully shaking his dark head as he began moving slowly across the carpet towards her.

'Don't start celebrating too soon,' Kate warned him, tension sharpening her voice as she backed nervously away from his advancing figure. 'Helen clearly doesn't believe either of us . . . and neither would I, if I'd darned nearly caught my boyfriend in a hot clinch with another woman! And while I'm on the subject—what on earth did you think you were doing, forcing yourself on me like that?'

'Oh, I was forcing myself on you, was I?' Dominic raised a dark, quizzical eyebrow. 'And what about *your* conduct last night, Miss Macaulay?' he drawled sardonically. 'I don't recall any strong protest on your part—rather the reverse, in fact!'

It was a low blow beneath the belt, and they both knew it. Kate's cheeks flushed a deep crimson as she scowled up at him.

'You really are the pits!' she ground out, helplessly trying to cudgel her brains for a rational, sensible reason for her extraordinary behaviour last night. Unfortunately, the close proximity of his tall figure seemed to be affecting her ability to think clearly.

'I was just ... well, I was just taken by surprise, that's all,' she muttered lamely, her embarrassment and chagrin increasing as Dominic responded to her words with a low, cynical laugh.

'Taken by surprise...?' he mocked cruelly, before stepping forward and pulling her unresisting body into his arms. 'To say that you took *me* by surprise last night is the understatement of the year!' he murmured, before lowering his dark head towards her.

'No...please...I...' Kate wasn't able to say anything more, her words cut short as his mouth possessed her trembling lips, his arms tightening like bands of steel, moulding her firmly to the hard length of his muscular body.

Almost faint with dizziness, Kate felt her heart begin thumping in a crazy, uneven rhythm beneath the devastating effect of his kiss, the compelling, sensual arousal of his lips and tongue provoking an ardent and passionate response, over which she appeared to have no control as she moaned helplessly in his arms.

Dominic's lips seemed to linger reluctantly as they left her mouth, trailing down to the wildly beating pulse at the base of her throat. Slowly raising his head, he gazed down at her with an enigmatic gleam in his clear blue eyes.

As she surfaced slowly from a deep mist of desire, Kate's eyelids fluttered rapidly while she stared blindly up at him, her limbs shaking and trembling as if in the grip of a raging fever. A moment later, a deep crimson flush swept over her cheeks as she realised just how her treacherous body had once again betrayed her.

'Well, now, I don't think that *very* interesting kiss comes under the heading of undue force, do you?' Dominic murmured, his lips curving into a sardonic grin as he released her and took a step backwards.

'You...you horrible man—you're engaged to be married. You've no right to go around kissing strange girls!' Kate gasped in a strangled voice as she tried to pull her scattered wits together.

His shoulders shook with amusement. 'You may have a point there,' he agreed. 'Because you are definitely the strangest girl I've ever come across!' he added in a soft murmur, lowering his head to gently brush his mouth across her trembling lips, before turning on his heel and striding over to the door.

'I hate you, Dominic Smith-Farrell!' Kate yelled, almost dancing with rage as he swiftly left the room. 'I *really* hate and despise you!'

But, if he heard her words, he gave no sign. Only the sound of his cynical, ironic laughter echoed down the corridor behind him.

CHAPTER SIX

AFTER Dominic had left the room, it took Kate quite a long time to simmer down. However, it was clearly going to be a gloriously hot, sunny day. So, unless she was going to stay sulking up here in her bedroom, she might as well try and make an effort to pull herself together.

Climbing into a clean pair of jeans, she was just pulling a thin blue and white striped T-shirt over her head when Alice knocked and came into the room.

'I've never known anyone who can vanish into thin air the way you do,' Kate grinned at the girl.

'When you were having your shower, Dom came in and told me to make myself scarce,' Alice explained. 'So I thought...'

'He just wanted to...er...talk about the arrangements for the mock battle,' Kate lied quickly. She didn't like not telling the truth, but there was no way she could explain the complicated situation between herself and Dominic—and certainly not to his young sister. 'So if you don't mind waiting for a minute, while I brush my hair,' she added, 'I guess I'll take you up on that offer to show me around the house.'

'Who's that guy?' Kate asked some time later, as she and Alice strolled slowly down the long picture gallery, running the whole length of the house on the upper floor.

'Don't you know?' Alice turned to look at her with shocked, incredulous eyes. 'That's King Charles the First, of course!'

'Oh, yes—of course,' Kate echoed quickly. But the younger girl clearly wasn't fooled.

'You'd better mug up on your English history—especially now that you're going to help arrange our Civil War battle,' Alice warned her. 'King Charles the First is an important part of our family tradition. In fact, his visit here for a few nights, before he surrendered to the Scottish army, is just about Thornton Priory's only claim to fame.'

'OK, I've got it now,' Kate clicked her fingers. 'He was the guy who was beheaded by the Roundheads, right? Does his ghost walk up and down this gallery, with his head tucked beneath his arm?'

Alice gave a heavy sigh. 'Yes, the King did lose his head. But he was executed in London, so he's not likely to haunt a house in Norfolk, is he?'

'No, I guess not,' Kate muttered, disappointed that the family didn't have a tame ghost. 'The King really stayed here, huh?'

'Oh, yes. And we've got his nightcap—although so have lots of other houses, I'm afraid. Wherever he stayed, the King seems to have left half his clothes behind him,' Alice explained, a note of grievance in her voice. 'But we've also got his prayer book, a pair of his gloves, and over here...' She caught hold of Kate's hand, and dragged her over to a glass case. 'Here, we've got a letter from the King, in which he promises to pay for the horses and food which he took away with him. Not that he ever did, of course,' she added with a shrug.

Kate gazed at the yellowing piece of parchment, trying to make sense of the thin black spidery writing. No wonder Alice was so proud of the family's relics! Even she, a complete stranger to the house, felt a thrill of excitement at the sight of that three-hundred-and-fifty-year-old piece of living history.

'What was King Charles doing here?' she asked, going over to sit down on a padded seat set in the curve of a mullioned window.

'Well, it was towards the end of the Civil War—the King and the Cavaliers, versus Oliver Cromwell, Parliament and the Roundheads,' Alice began as she came to sit down beside Kate. 'Poor old King Charles and his armies had just about lost every battle by then, and he was stuck in Oxford, with Cromwell and the Parliamentary forces closing in on him.'

'That sounds a bit tricky.'

'Yes, it was,' Alice agreed, explaining how the King had eventually decided to escape from Oxford and join the Scottish army—who were opposed to Cromwell, mainly because of religious differences—intending to play one army off against the other. Heavily disguised, the King and two companions made their way across England to the seaport of King's Lynn, hoping to take a boat up the east coast to Scotland. Unfortunately, by the time they arrived in Norfolk, the Scottish army had marched down through England and were camped at Newark. 'Which lies diagonally across the Wash from where we are now,' Alice added. 'Got it so far?'

'Yes, I guess so. King's Lynn is only a few miles away from here, isn't it?' Kate said, recalling the road map she had studied for her journey to Thornton Priory.

'That's right,' Alice nodded, going on to relate how the King had stayed in the house for some days, before eventually deciding that he had no alternative but to surrender to the Scots. The family had given him horses, food and a change of clothing, before he travelled across the Fens towards Cambridgeshire and on to Newark—and to his eventual imprisonment and death.

'The family—we were only Farrells then, of course—got into quite a lot of trouble for helping the King,' Alice explained. 'But luckily Sir William Farrell had escaped abroad earlier in the war, and his children were too young to be put in prison.'

'Hey, that's really interesting,' Kate exclaimed. 'I had no idea that this house was so famous.'

'Well, it's not really all *that* famous,' Alice admitted regretfully. 'King Charles did stay in an awful lot of houses, although I think he must have though Lady Farrell was quite pretty—don't you?' she asked, getting up and going over to point up at a large portrait on the wall.

'Yes, she is lovely,' Kate agreed, staring up at the portrait of a beautiful woman wearing a low-cut, deep blue satin gown, whose bodice was covered with thick flounces of heavy lace. Large, translucent pearls were wound through her fair hair, and Kate couldn't help feeling that she'd seen the picture of the woman before, somewhere.

'It's a super dress, isn't it?' Alice was saying as Kate continued to gaze at the portrait with puzzled eyes. 'I wish I had a dress like that.'

'It would certainly look better on you than the sort of thing you're wearing at the moment,' Kate agreed, feeling that this was the perfect opportunity to try and do something positive about the young girl's bizarre clothing. 'I don't feel that black and sludge-green are exactly your colours, somehow,' she added carefully.

Alice shrugged. 'No, I know they aren't. And in fact ...' She was interrupted as Kate gave a sudden yelp.

'How stupid of me!' she cried, clicking her fingers with annoyance. 'I *knew* I'd seen her somewhere. It's you, of course!'

'What ...?' Alice looked at her in alarm. 'Are you feeling all right?'

'As right as rain,' Kate laughed, taking hold of the girl's shoulders and turning her around to stand facing the portrait. 'Now, take a real good look,' she commanded. 'Of course, this woman is a lot older than you, but I'm darn sure that in a few years' time you're going to turn out to be her spitting image.'

'Really?'

'Really and truly!' Kate promised her with a beaming smile. 'So I reckon it's about time you stopped being a caterpillar in these awful dresses, and began getting ready to be transformed into a beautiful butterfly.'

Alice was clearly thrilled at the idea of becoming as lovely as the lady in the portrait, and more than willing to listen to some sound advice.

'Look, I think it's time you stopped worrying about other members of your family, and concentrated on yourself. It's a crying shame for a girl of your age to be going around looking like an old hag!' Kate told her bluntly.

'Maybe you're right, but...'

'I need to buy some more clothes myself, so why don't we both go in to the nearest town and have a shopping spree? I'm not going to try and twist your arm, of course,' Kate added quickly. 'But I reckon a brand-new pair of jeans might prove pretty useful, eh?'

'Levi 501s?' Alice asked hopefully.

'Sure—why not?' Kate shrugged, turning away to hide a smile as she realised that kids were the same the world over.

'They're awfully expensive. Are you sure you can afford it?' Alice asked anxiously.

'I reckon I'm good for a pair—and a T-shirt or two as well,' Kate assured her solemnly. 'However, there is just one catch, I'm afraid. The fact is that while I like you a lot, kid, there's no way I'm taking you shopping in either those awful clothes you're wearing—or that hideous make-up!'

Alice laughed. 'That's no problem! I'll just dash off and get changed,' she added, before running off down the gallery and quickly disappearing from view.

It really was her idea of heaven. With the wind flowing through her hair, no sound other than the noise of pounding hoofs and the powerful, muscular strength of the horse beneath her as she galloped across the park, Kate found herself laughing out loud with sheer joy and exhilaration.

Although the weekend here in Norfolk had started so badly, things definitely seemed to be looking up, she thought, briefly turning her head to smile at the rider behind her, before gradually bringing her horse to a halt.

'That was really *great*!' she called out breathlessly as Dominic rode up to join her.

He laughed. 'You may drive me up the wall much of the time, but I'll say this for you, Kate—you certainly know how to ride a horse!'

'Well, I ought to,' she retorted. 'Dad always said I was practically born in the saddle. And we'll have less of the insults, if you don't mind,' she added with a grin. 'I'm in far too good a mood to put up with any more arguments.'

'Ah, yes, we mustn't forget our pact, must we?'

'Absolutely not,' she agreed, reining in her horse as he leant down to open a five-barred gate set in the park wall, before leading the way down a small country lane.

It really was a stroke of luck that had brought Dominic to the stables after all the family had attended church this morning. Kate had admired the ancient building with its brass plaques and the old monuments bearing carved stone effigies of former members of the Farrell family. She had also been impressed by the way that Dominic had read the lesson from the Old Testament.

'I'd have been terrified of mispronouncing some of those difficult old Hebrew names,' she told him with a grin, when he'd discovered her admiring the horses in the stable.

'You're quite right. When I was younger, I used to be certain I was going to make a complete fool of myself,' he'd told her with a smile, before glancing down at her slim jeans topped by a thin silk blouse. 'I see you've changed out of the dress you were wearing for church. Would you like to come for a short ride with me?'

'I'd love to,' she had agreed enthusiastically, then was immediately assailed by second thoughts on the subject. 'But only if you promise not to quarrel with me,' she added cautiously.

Dominic had laughed. 'I was just about to make the same point. So I suggest that we make a pact: no arguments!'

'You're on!' Kate had agreed, before saddling up the animal chosen for her by Dominic, and a few minutes later they were riding slowly out of the stable yard.

Who could have guessed, after their disastrous encounter in her bedroom yesterday morning, that Dominic would now be acting in such a companionable, friendly way towards her? Maybe the absence of Helen, who had apparently gone to spend the morning with her father, had something to do with it. Or possibly the sudden magical transformation in Alice's appearance had led to him being in such an amiable mood?

After Alice had readily agreed to accompany Kate on a shopping spree, they had been offered a lift by Aunt Laura, who had already arranged to take Martin that afternoon into the neighbouring town of King's Lynn.

As she now followed Dominic through the five-barred gate, Kate grinned to herself as she recalled how Alice had practically 'gone ape' in one of King's Lynn's department stores. Leaping excitedly from counter to counter as she grabbed a handful of blue jeans and T-shirts, the girl had dashed into the changing-rooms, emerging some time later with an ecstatic smile on her face—and looking a completely different person!

'Hey, that's terrific!' Kate had exclaimed, gazing in amazement at the fresh-scrubbed, neat and tidy, stunning-looking girl standing in front of her.

'Are you sure it's all right for me to have these clothes?' Alice had asked anxiously. 'I'm sure they must be costing you a lot of money...?'

'I can tell you, kid, it's definitely worth every penny,' Kate assured her fervently. 'Come on, let's go and give your mother and Martin the shock of their lives!'

'Are we going anywhere in particular?' she asked as she rode, now, down the lane beside Dominic.

'Yes, I have to call on one of my farm tenants. He's thinking of installing a new pig unit, and he wants to talk to me about it. However, you may be more interested in Mr Lacey's main occupation—when he isn't farming, of course. He breeds and shows champion gun-dogs.'

'I'd love to see them,' Kate agreed. 'I used to have an old sheepdog. Ben was such a great fellow, and it nearly broke my heart to have to get rid of him when I sold the farm. But there was no way I could keep him in a town or city—not after he'd had the run of the homestead. I found him a good home, of course,' she added, smiling mistily up at Dominic. 'But I still miss him very much.'

'What a surprising girl you are, Kate,' he said quietly. 'You appear to be so strong and confident on the surface, but I suspect you're remarkably uncertain and vulnerable underneath.'

'Pure marshmallow,' she agreed with a wry grin. 'But then I don't reckon you're quite as hard and tough as you make out, either.'

'Oh, yes, I am!' He gave a harsh bark of sardonic laughter. 'Unfortunately, in my profession, I see so many rogues and crooked businessmen that it's sometimes hard to remember that not everyone has criminal tendencies.'

'Like when you first met me, you mean?'

He laughed again. 'Now, Kate, don't spoil a peaceful day by reminding me of an episode I would much rather forget!'

'I guess that goes for me too,' she agreed, looking around her with interest as they turned off the lane and rode towards a white-painted farmhouse, surrounded on three sides by a large yard full of farm implements.

While Dominic conferred with the farmer, Robert Lacey, Kate was shown over the kennels by the farmer's wife. Mrs Lacey was a small, plump woman who was clearly devoted to their dogs.

'Don't get me wrong,' Kate said as Mrs Lacey placed a small puppy in her arms. 'But these animals...'

'They're black Labradors, dearie.'

'Yes, well... this puppy's mother, for instance, seems to be a bit on the small side for a gun-dog, if you know what I mean?'

Mrs Lacey chuckled. 'Ah, but that's because they're from the Sandringham strain. The Queen breeds black Labradors at Sandringham, here in Norfolk—and she's produced many a Field Trial champion too. They're on the small side, I agree, but they're great gun-dogs and hardly have to be trained, because they instinctively seem to know it all,' she enthused, before nodding towards the puppy Kate was holding. 'Mr Smith-Farrell has bought that little fellow, and we reckon he's got a right good 'un!'

'Ah, I see my wife has been showing you around the kennels,' Mr Lacey said with a broad smile, as he and Dominic walked across the farmyard towards them.

'It's about time you collected your puppy,' Mrs Lacey told Dominic.

'I know.' He grinned at her. 'But unfortunately I've got a case coming up in Hong Kong. So you'll have to hang on to him for a bit, I'm afraid.'

'I can look after the puppy for you while you're away,' Kate said impulsively. 'Do let's take him with us,' she urged.

'No, he's still very young. I think it's best that we leave him here for a few more weeks.'

'Oh, Dominic . . . *please*!'

'No, Kate—absolutely not!'

As they rode slowly homewards, Dominic looked at Kate with exasperation. 'I don't know what's come over me—I must be losing my mind.' He shook his head ruefully. 'Is the puppy all right?'

'Sure—he seems to be fine,' Kate smiled down at the small creature, tucked into the folds of her sweater, which she was wearing tied about her waist. 'He really is a cute little dog. And I don't think you're losing your mind. You're just proving that you can be a regular guy, after all.' She laughed as he pulled a face. 'Besides, I just bet Alice is going to be crazy about him!'

'If I know my sister, that dog will undoubtedly be thoroughly spoiled,' Dominic agreed with a laugh. 'And, speaking of Alice—I gather it's you whom I have to thank for persuading her to stop wearing those utterly vile clothes. How on earth did you do it?'

Kate shrugged. 'Well, it wasn't too hard. Not once I'd figured out why she was wearing them in the first place.'

'Why *was* she so determined to go around looking like the Bride of Dracula?'

'Ah...well...' Kate hesitated for a moment. 'I'm not at all sure you'll like the answer to that question.'

'Nevertheless, I want to hear it,' he said firmly.

'OK—but don't say you haven't been warned,' she told him bluntly, before relating the pathetic attempt by his young sister to put Helen off the idea of marrying him. 'It's really a very sad little story,' Kate added. 'And, before you start getting cross with me, I can assure you I have pointed out to Alice—very firmly indeed—that she really must not try, ever again, to interfere in your love-life.'

Dominic's expression had grown hard and flinty while he listened to Kate's explanation. Now he made no effort to break the silence between them, continuing to ride quietly beside her, clearly buried deep in his own thoughts. And there was no way she intended to break the silence, Kate thought nervously. She'd been very careful not to be too rude about Horrid Helen. However, even if he was besotted with love for his fiancée, Dominic could hardly fail to see that his family felt very differently about the girl he was planning to marry. *Not* a happy scene!

'I can't...er...pretend to be pleased about what you've just told me,' he said flatly, breaking the silence at last. 'However, I suppose I ought to be grateful that Alice felt she could turn to you. Although I fail to understand why she didn't tell me herself how she felt about...er...the situation,' he added with a distinct note of annoyance in his voice.

'Oh, come on!' Kate felt stung into rushing to Alice's defence. 'The kid's only sixteen, for heaven's sake. She was bound to think that you'd never listen to her. Quite frankly, I don't think you would have, either.'

'When I want your opinion I'll ask for it!' he informed her coldly.

'Oh, great! I just knew I'd get it in the neck, one way or another. Bearers of bad tidings always do, don't they?' she muttered gloomily. 'Well, it's not my fault that your family can't stand Horrid Helen, is it?'

'Don't call her that!' he grated.

'Why not—everyone else does,' Kate said defiantly. 'The fact is, you don't appear to have any idea of how your brother and sister feel about things. And poor Aunt Laura seems to be in a bit of a state as well.'

'What nonsense!' Dominic retorted, his hands tightening on the reins, causing his horse to check and nearly stumble on the hard ground. 'You must be out of your mind!'

She gave a shrill laugh. 'If anyone's nuts around here, it certainly isn't me, buddy!'

'Let's get one thing straight, Kate,' he snarled as he quickly collected his horse. 'I don't mind what else you call me, but I utterly refuse to be referred to as buddy. Do I make myself clear?'

'OK—OK, stay cool, man,' she muttered quickly.

He shuddered. 'That's not much better, but I don't suppose I'd better press my luck!'

Kate risked a slanting, sideways glance at him through her eyelashes, and was surprised to see his mouth twitching with grim humour.

'You're quite correct,' he said at last. 'I do seem to have been taking my annoyance out on you, and I apologise for doing so. However, I really think you must explain your veiled references to stress and strain in my family.'

'No way! You'll only be mad as a hornet with me.'

Dominic turned his dark head to give her a wry smile. 'All I can say is that I'll try to "stay cool".'

Kate thought hard for a moment. Despite what he'd just said, she knew he wouldn't like hearing the unvarnished truth. However, maybe it would be worth it, if only for the family's sake. Neither she nor they might ever get a chance like this again.

'Well . . .' she took a deep breath, 'I really don't agree with Alice. She seems to think you're the cleverest thing on two legs, and she's also convinced that you know all about everything that goes on at the Priory. But, as far as I'm concerned, I reckon you're as blind as a bat!'

'What on earth are you talking about?'

'I'm talking about Martin, for instance,' she replied coolly. 'I've only just met my cousin, but even *I* know that the boy hates the idea of going to university. All he's ever wanted to do is to become a farmer and help you here on the estate.' She shrugged. 'However, it looks as if that's just too bad, because you seem to have made your mind up about what's best for him. Right?

'And as for Alice...' she continued quickly, 'if she *had* been able to confide in you—as she ought to have been able to do—you'd have known that all those crazy clothes and weird make-up were purely a result of her unhappiness at your engagement to Helen.'

'Anything more?' he queried acidly as they rode back into the stable yard of the Priory. 'Any other little item about my family, on which you have strong views?'

'No, I...er...I think that's about it,' she muttered, feeling she had said more than enough for one day.

'I can't think where you get your quite extraordinary ideas from,' he said angrily, before vaulting down from his large chestnut horse and coming over to carefully take the puppy from her hands.

'OK, fine—forget I said anything,' Kate shrugged, getting down from her horse and leading it across the cobbled stone floor of the stables.

'You've hardly been in the house for a day, and yet you already seem to regard yourself as an expert on the family. You've even got the brass nerve to try and give me a lecture about my own brother and sister,' he muttered bitterly.

'Oh, dear, here we go,' she said with a heavy, dramatic sigh. 'I just knew it was too good to last!'

'What are you talking about?' He frowned, putting the puppy down in a box of straw and following her as she led her horse into its stall.

'I thought we had a pact? No arguments, remember? And if I've said anything about my cousins which you don't like, then you ought to remember that you insisted on hearing what I had to say.'

'An opportunity which you seized with both hands!' he pointed out grimly.

'Yes, I'm afraid you're quite right!' Removing her horse's bridle, Kate turned and gave him a bright smile, which she hoped he would find extremely irritating.

Dominic closed his eyes for a moment, taking a deep breath before grinding out through clenched teeth, 'Believe me, Kate, there are times when I could—quite cheerfully—wring your neck!'

'Yes, I know.' She grinned. 'But I'm determined to try and keep to our pact. For one thing, I'm thrilled about the puppy. And for another... er... um...' She hesitated, forgetting what she had been going to say as he began moving purposefully towards her.

'Cut it out, Dominic!' she muttered uneasily, backing away until she bumped up against the horse, who was by now contentedly munching his hay. 'And it's no good you standing there trying to look dark and dangerous, because I... well, I reckon you're nothing but a big softy at heart.'

'A big softy...? What a revolting description!' He grimaced with disgust.

'Oh yes, you are. I reckon you're a pushover as far as that little puppy is concerned. And I'm sure it won't be more than a couple of days before *you're* the one who's taking it walkies!'

Dominic stared down at her intently for a moment. 'But only a few minutes ago you were accusing me of being cruel and heedless towards my brother and sister,' he said, his voice heavy with cynical amusement. 'You really can't have it both ways, Kate.'

'Oh, yes, I can!' she retorted quickly, well aware that she was being childish, but completely unable to think of a fast sophisticated answer. Quite amazingly, her mind appeared to have become a mass of dense cotton wool, and there must surely be something wrong with her lungs? Because she seemed to be having great difficulty in breathing properly.

Unable to prevent a wild surge of colour flooding over her cheeks as Dominic leaned closer, she looked past him towards the door of the stable, trying to focus on something—anything!—that would allow her to evade the disturbing glint in his gleaming blue eyes.

'Go away!' she muttered helplessly as he moved closer to her trembling body, trying to inch away past the heavy, compact body of the horse. But he merely gave a low, husky laugh that sent shivers fizzing up and down her backbone.

'No, I don't think so,' he murmured silkily. 'I rather like the idea of being "dark and dangerous"!' He gave another deep, husky chuckle. 'Is that really how you see me, Kate?'

'No, of course not,' she gasped, trembling as she felt the heat and power of his body against her own. 'I was just . . . er . . . just joking,' she added desperately, trying to stop her shaking legs from buckling at the knees.

'Hmm . . . that's a pity,' he whispered softly, and there seemed nothing she could do as he slowly lowered his dark head towards her. Through her thin silk shirt she could feel his heart pounding in unison with her own hectic pulse beats; the warmth of his breath against her cheek sending *frissons* of excitement zigzagging through her body.

Everything appeared to be happening in slow motion. It was as though time had no meaning; hours in which to tell herself, Oh, goodness, he's going to kiss me again! . . . Long minutes when she could have easily escaped from beneath the tall figure pinning her lightly to the warm, heavy body of the horse. But it seemed that there was nothing she could do other than to stare mesmerised up at his face, now so close to her own that she was aware of his thickly fringed black eyelashes, and the faint flush beneath his smoothly tanned skin.

And then their mindless state was abruptly shattered by the sound of a strident, imperious voice calling out in the distance.

'Dominic? Where are you?'

He groaned, swearing softly under his breath as he quickly released her trembling figure. Momentarily paralysed, Kate took a second or two before she managed to pull her scattered wits together.

'Horrid Helen strikes again!' she muttered shakily, desperately trying to control her ragged breathing and the heavy pounding of her heart.

'I've told you to stop calling her by that stupid name!' he rasped.

With one part of her dazed mind, Kate knew that he was merely giving vent to his frustrated emotions. But she had enough problems of her own to cope with—and it was about time Dominic realised he couldn't keep playing both ends against the middle.

'Well, don't just stand there,' she said bitterly. 'It sounds as though your dear fiancée is on the prowl. So why don't you be a good little boy and run along to see what she wants?'

He swore violently under his breath. 'I wish to God I'd never set eyes on you!' he hissed savagely, his face pale and strained in the dim light of the stable block.

'Don't worry, *buddy*,' Kate snarled back. 'The feeling is entirely mutual!'

And, quickly turning away to hide the foolish, weak tears filling her eyes, she took to her heels and ran blindly across the old stable yard, towards the back door of the Priory.

CHAPTER SEVEN

MUCH later that night as she sat by her bedroom window, Kate gave a heavy sigh. Gazing down at the rose garden and lawns bathed in an eerie silvery light from the full moon, she couldn't help thinking that this place would be *so* idyllic, if it weren't for the complications of her relationship with Dominic.

Unlike Helen, who seemed to value the Priory mainly for the status it would give her as Dominic's wife, Kate was coming to love the fascinating old building for its own sake; for the timeless atmosphere of its mellow bricks, and the deep sense of peace and stability in an otherwise fast and ever-changing world. In fact, she couldn't think of anything nicer than living in a house which was so obviously steeped in history.

Moreover, she was really enjoying the companionship of her new cousins, and Aunt Laura had also proved to be very kind and welcoming. But... and it was a large 'but'... interesting as the house and her new family might be, everything seemed to pale into insignificance beside the magnitude of her present problem. Because, if she didn't watch out—*there appeared to be a very real danger that she might be falling in love with Dominic Smith-Farrell!*

How could it be happening to her? The extraordinary emotional turmoil which seemed to have her in thrall simply didn't make any kind of sense.

Goodness knows, she'd tried telling herself it was only a case of sex rearing its ugly head—or that she was simply looking for a new romance, on the rebound from that smoothie, Charles Yorke. But none of those sensible arguments seemed to make a blind bit of difference, she thought miserably. What on earth had she ever done to deserve such an ill-fated and clearly doom-ridden response to the horrid man?

Of course, it was no good trying to pretend it was all one-sided—a figment of her overheated imagination. Because she'd have to be blind, deaf and dumb not to know that Dominic was equally attracted to her. So maybe he was asking himself the same questions? Could he too be as confused and upset as she was? Or were men used to coping with these sort of violent emotions? Not for the first time, Kate wished she'd had more experience of the opposite sex.

Quite apart from anything else, she still failed to see why he had ever got engaged to Helen in the first place. Even if the English girl was the daughter of his godfather, and therefore a very suitable choice for a wife, the whole relationship really didn't make much sense. Dominic had obviously been shattered to discover why Alice had been wearing all those terrible clothes. But even if he'd been fooled at first, surely he ought to have seen through Helen by now?

Oh, yeah? Isn't it about time you stopped kidding yourself? Kate gave a mirthless, grim laugh, remembering how from her window she'd seen Dominic kissing Helen before helping her into his car to catch the train back to London.

It didn't really matter how obnoxious Helen might be; *any* man would almost certainly fall like a ton of bricks for such an outstandingly beautiful, sophisticated woman. And you're hardly what Helen would regard as serious competition, she told herself, staring unhappily at her reflection in the mirror.

However, she really must make a determined effort to try and pull herself together. Of course, it was probably the whole uncertainty and confusion of her relationship with Dominic which was making her feel so depressed. And maybe it was a mistake, after their disastrous quarrel in the stable, to have spent so much time hiding up here in her bedroom? As a result, she'd spent too many long, solitary hours with nothing to do but think about her problems—a situation not helped by avoiding the need to join the rest of the family at dinner, with the excuse that she had a bad headache.

Which wasn't too far from the truth, she acknowledged grimly. As far as she was concerned, Dominic was becoming one large headache. What *was* it about the damn man? Why should her legs turn to jelly, and her heart begin to thump and pound like a sledgehammer, every time they were anywhere near each other? Was it really true love? Or was it some sort of mad infatuation, which would rapidly burn itself out in time?

It was a question to which she still hadn't found an answer. And, as she struggled to come to terms with her errant emotions—falling in love with Dominic would definitely be a fate worse than death!—she became aware of a distant sound, like the cry of a small child.

Frowning in puzzlement—surely it couldn't possibly be Alice, whose bedroom was in a far wing of the enormous house?—Kate slowly realised that the faint noise was coming from the kitchen, which lay directly beneath her room. A few minutes later, finding herself completely unable to ignore the muffled, heartrending sound, she slipped on a thin wrap and opened her bedroom door. Tiptoeing silently down the large staircase and on through the massive space of the dark and empty hall, she went into the kitchen.

'Oh, you poor darling!' she exclaimed, crossing the dimly lit room to pick up the small puppy, who was moaning piteously from a cardboard box beside the large stove. 'Are you crying for your mother...?' she murmured softly as the small creature shivered in her arms. 'Never mind, sweetie, you can come upstairs to bed with me.'

'Now that's an invitation I'd be happy to accept!' The deep voice issuing from the dark shadows across the room made her jump in fright. 'Unfortunately the puppy must stay in the kitchen, I'm afraid.'

'For crying out loud!' Kate gasped. 'What are you doing down here at this time of night?' she demanded breathlessly, frowning nervously at the tall figure of Dominic as he closed the kitchen door behind him.

'My dear Kate, I'm sorry to have to remind you that this *is* my house, and I can't help feeling I have a perfect right to come and go as I please,' he drawled blandly, walking forward to place two glasses and a bottle of whisky on the kitchen table.

'Yes, of course you have. I...er...you just gave me a shock, that's all,' she muttered, awkwardly trying to pull the edges of her gown closer together, without disturbing the small dog in her arms.

Dominic's mouth twitched in silent humour as he viewed Kate's attempt to preserve her modesty—a clear waste of time in view of that remarkably short, sketchy garment she was wearing over her thin silk nightgown. However, possibly this was not the moment to say so, or to mention his appreciation of her magnificent figure.

'I'm sorry if I gave you a fright,' he said. 'But the truth is, I couldn't get to sleep. I was just in my study, having a glass of whisky and trying to find something to read, when I heard the puppy crying.'

'Yes...well, I couldn't get to sleep either,' she admitted, trying not to stare at his tall figure clothed in a short towelling robe. She hadn't seen him face to face since that desperately upsetting scene in the stables. But she couldn't just pretend it hadn't happened, could she?

'I...er...I reckon I probably owe you an...er...an apology,' she began, glancing nervously down at her bare feet. 'I guess I didn't really mean half the nasty things I said this afternoon, and...'

'If anyone should apologise, it's undoubtedly me,' he said firmly. 'However, I think we should both try and wipe the whole scene from our minds, hmm?'

'Well...'

'Oh, for goodness' sake, Kate, why don't you stop standing there like a stag at bay, and come and sit down?' he snapped.

She hesitated for a moment, clutching the puppy tightly to her chest. 'Er... I don't know. It's kind of late, and...'

'Since we've both been disturbed by the noise of that puppy, we might as well relax and have a drink,' he told her with a smile. 'Or would you like some hot cocoa?'

'Yuk—no, thank you!' she grimaced. 'This "great hulk of a girl" definitely doesn't need all those extra calories!'

Dominic groaned. 'You're never going to let me forget that stupid remark of mine, are you?'

'You're so right,' she agreed, finding herself unable to suppress a grin as she gazed down at the rueful expression on his handsome face. 'I reckon it's going to be years and years before I let you off the hook.'

'Years...' He lifted a dark, sardonic eyebrow. 'I wonder if that's a promise or a threat?' And when she continued to stare silently back at him, feeling foolish and tongue-tied, he leaned back in his chair, regarding her with a lazy smile. 'Tell me, Kate, just how long do you see our future...er...relationship lasting?'

'It will be a miracle if it lasts beyond the next five seconds,' she muttered grimly, bitterly aware of the high tide of colour spreading over her cheeks. 'Here, you can look after him for a bit, while I find something to eat,' she added, quickly placing the small puppy in his lap.

'Hey! Wait a minute...'

'Too bad—I'm starving!' she called out over her shoulder as she hurried across the room towards a long range of cupboards.

Well, yes, it *was* true that she was hungry. In fact, now she came to think about it, it was all this man's fault that she had missed the evening meal. But her hunger was only an excuse—an imperative need to put some space between them.

What on earth had caused her to make such a stupid, careless remark just now? Of course there was no possibility of a future relationship with Dominic. Quite apart from the fact that he was engaged to another woman, the very idea was laughable. Or it would be, if she didn't seem to have temporarily lost her sense of humour.

There really was no justice in this world, she told herself grimly, bending down to examine the contents of the icebox, and desperately trying to ignore her flushed cheeks, and the nervous excitement flickering through her body. There ought to be *very* strict laws against allowing tall, handsome men to walk around late at night. And especially those wearing only a short, dark blue towelling robe over long, slim brown legs!

'What have you got there?' he queried as, unable to put it off any longer, she returned reluctantly to the table.

'What...?' Kate sat down, gazing with confusion at the plate in front of her. She must be losing her mind, because she had absolutely no idea what she'd put between those pieces of bread and butter. Shrugging her shoulders, she bit into the sandwich. 'It seems to be peanut butter and jelly,' she mumbled.

'Now it's my turn to say "yuk"!' he grinned, pouring some whisky into a glass and pushing it across the table towards her. 'And I'm sure it contains far more calories than a mug of cocoa.'

'Who cares? It's a great combination. You ought to try it some time,' she retorted, lifting her glass and tipping a hefty dose of alcohol down her throat.

'Hey, go easy with that!' Dominic cautioned. 'We both know you haven't much of a head for hard liquor.'

Kate gave a defiant laugh, throwing him a provocative glance through her eyelashes as she deliberately raised the glass to her lips again. 'I may not have a head for it,' she conceded. 'However, since you're bound to want to quarrel with me again, I guess I'm going to need all the anaesthetic I can get hold of. Right?'

There was a long silence as Dominic stared down at the small puppy in his arms, stroking it gently.

'I have no wish to quarrel with you. Quite the reverse, in fact,' he said quietly, raising his dark head to gaze intently at the girl sitting opposite him.

Kate flushed at the searching, intense gleam in his eyes, and her heart began racing out of control. She tore her gaze away, suddenly breathless and profoundly thankful that he couldn't see her knees knocking together beneath the table. She knew it was dangerous to remain down here in the kitchen. But, like a naughty child who had been told not to touch the matches, she couldn't seem to resist the temptation to play with fire.

'No...well, I don't want to fight with you either,' she admitted huskily.

He gave her a warm smile. 'So, despite the unfortunate beginning to our relationship, there's no reason why we can't become . . . er . . . good friends, is there?'

'Well . . .'

'Oh, come on, Kate! If I'm prepared to forgive the loss of a beloved car, and featuring as a star turn in the headlines of a London newspaper, I don't see why you can't meet me halfway!'

Kate laughed. Sitting here in the warm, dimly lit kitchen, she was vibrantly aware of Dominic's gleaming blue eyes and the wry, amused smile on his hard mouth. It might well be the effect of the whisky zinging through her veins, but, quite unexpectedly, she suddenly felt extraordinarily cheerful and happy.

'I don't know about that,' she mocked, pushing a hand through her long tawny hair. 'Don't you think that becoming friends might be taking things just a little *too* far?'

'Surely it depends on how far you want to go?' he drawled silkily.

Kate swallowed nervously as she registered the smooth, sexy note in his voice. She'd better watch out. This conversation seemed to be getting rapidly out of hand!

Taking a deep breath, she said firmly, 'OK, lawyer-man. If we're going to be friends, maybe you'd better start by telling me something about yourself. How you and your family come to be living in this lovely old house, for instance? I enjoyed riding over part of the estate today, and I've had a sketchy history lesson from Alice, but that's about all.'

'It's not a particularly exciting story. But if you're really interested . . . ?'

'Yes, of course I am. So shoot!'

Resting her chin on her hand, Kate listened as he talked; interested at first, and then gradually becoming enthralled as he filled in the gaps of the brief information she had gathered from Alice and Aunt Laura.

As the tale unfolded, it appeared that his father, whose family had owned the Priory for hundreds of years, had married a beautiful and very wealthy Spanish girl. An only child, she had lost both her parents in a car accident soon after she was born, leaving her with no relatives other than an aged great-aunt who lived in London.

'I hardly remember my mother,' Dominic said sadly. 'Just sometimes, when I catch the scent of the perfume she always used to wear, then I can recall some brief scenes from my childhood. Her death in the fire here at the Priory was a terrible blow to my father, and one from which I don't think he ever recovered. Although Laura certainly made him as happy as he could ever hope to be,' Dominic added, going on to explain that his inheritance from his mother did seem at times to be a heavy burden.

'I certainly don't need such a large house in London. However, before he died, my father made me promise not to sell the property, or to dismiss Mr and Mrs Lewis, who had always worked for my mother's family. So that's one white elephant which has to be maintained—and this house is another,' he added with a wry grin.

Kate certainly hadn't appreciated the problems involved in the maintenance of a minor stately home. 'If it isn't the roof which needs mending, then you can be very sure there'll be dry rot somewhere,' Dominic told her ruefully. 'While the estate just about pays for itself, this house is a constant drain on my resources.' Which was why, as he further explained, he had to work so hard in London, earning as much money as he could in his profession as a barrister.

Kate gave him a puzzled frown. 'I realise that the legal system in this country is somewhat different from that in Canada and the States. But I don't understand your connection with Hong Kong?'

'There's an important commercial trial coming up there.' He grimaced slightly. 'I really didn't want the job, so I instructed my clerk to ask for a fee of a million pounds.'

'Wow!' Kate whistled.

Dominic shrugged his broad shoulders. 'I thought that would be the end of the matter, but unfortunately, the whole business seems to have boomeranged back on me. The clients apparently want my services, and have agreed to pay the money. I'm not complaining, of course, but there are times when I think the world is going crazy,' he added with a sigh.

'Well, I guess you must be good at your job—and let's face it, that sort of money has to be pretty useful. Especially if, as you say, this house seems to swallow up all you earn,' Kate added. 'But it does sound as if you've got yourself on a bit of a treadmill, doesn't it?'

He stared down at the pale golden liquid in his glass. 'Yes, you're right,' he agreed slowly. 'It may be immodest to say so, but I am good at my job and I have, I hope, a fairly long career ahead of me. However, my present high-powered and at times frantic lifestyle doesn't leave me with much time to deal with either matters on the estate, or what seem to be increasing family problems.'

As Dominic gave a heavy sigh, thrusting a hand roughly through his dark hair, Kate was shaken to the core by confused feelings of love, warmth and sympathy. It was an emotional response she didn't quite know how to handle, especially when applied to a man she had always thought of as being so hard, tough and arrogant. He really did seem to have had a lot of responsibilities placed on his shoulders; burdens which he had been forced to bear from a very early age. I'm lucky, she told herself. I've only got myself to worry about. I honestly don't know how I'd have coped with running this house and the estate, as well as having to look after a young half-brother and sister—or a stepmother who's as scatty as Aunt Laura...

Buried in thought as she strove to readjust some of her views of the man sitting across the table, it was a few moments before Kate realised he was still discussing his family problems.

'...Thanks to you, Alice seems to be turning back into an ordinary teenager—I wasn't sure just how long I could stand those terrible, vampire-type clothes!' Dominic gave her a warm smile. 'And I've taken note of the points you made earlier today about Martin wanting to be a farmer. I'll admit that I'd still like him to go to university, but maybe he'll accept a compromise and agree to go to an agricultural college.'

'That sounds a good idea,' she murmured, still feeling slightly bemused. She hadn't thought about it before, but it must be tough having to be the titular head of the family. Aunt Laura was a dear, of course, but she clearly wasn't up to providing much help and support—not even as far as her own children were concerned. Nor could her aunt be relied upon to take firm, positive decisions about the running of the house and the estate.

In fact, it was becoming obvious that what Dominic really needed was to have someone up here in Norfolk running the show and getting things organised. Especially when he was so heavily involved with his legal commitments, both in London and abroad. Which explained why he'd grabbed her help with the mock battle. And that *must* be the reason why...? Yes, of course! It had to be the answer, she told herself, as the pieces of the jigsaw which she had found so puzzling now fell neatly into place.

'I couldn't work it out before, but *now* I can see why you decided to marry Helen,' she exclaimed impulsively. 'She must have seemed the perfect choice if you wanted to get this place running on well-oiled wheels, right? And of course, I don't suppose you had any idea, when you first got engaged, just how awful and what a pain in the neck she really is! In fact, I...er... *Oh, dear...!*'

Kate's voice trailed away, her cheeks reddening as she glimpsed Dominic's taut, strained expression; the dark brows drawn together over his cold blue eyes in an angry frown.

'Whoops! I'm really sorry—I shouldn't have said that. I know I'm way out of line,' she muttered quickly, nervously seizing her glass and tipping the remaining liquid down her throat.

'Yes, you are. Pouring you that whisky was clearly a bad mistake,' he drawled in an icy, crushing tone of voice as he rose from the table. 'I can't see any point in prolonging this conversation, can you?'

'I have *not* had too much to drink!' Kate bristled, bitterly aware that she alone was responsible for destroying the warmth and companionship which had existed so briefly between them. Why on earth couldn't she learn to keep her stupid mouth shut?

'It's not my fault you're so super-sensitive about your rotten fiancée,' she grumbled. 'And what are you going to do about the puppy?'

'Nothing,' he snapped. 'It will be perfectly all right down here in the kitchen. Just be thankful that I'm not putting it outside in the cold, dark kennels with the other gun-dogs.'

'How can you be so heartless?' she cried, jumping to her feet and rushing over to snatch the sleepy puppy from his arms.

Dominic sighed and shook his head. 'For heaven's sake! Do stop being such an idiot!'

'I'm an idiot all right! Just when I was beginning to think you were a nice guy after all, I find out that you're the sort of person who's cruel to dumb animals,' she exclaimed bitterly.

'May the Lord give me patience!' he groaned. 'Now listen to me, Kate. If you put the little chap down in the box by the stove, he'll go off fast to sleep. It may seem cruel,' he added, moving towards her as she clasped the puppy to her bosom, 'but I can assure you it really is the kindest way in the long run.'

Maybe it was the whisky, still flowing strongly through her veins? Perhaps it was the close proximity of his tall, lithe body, or maybe she was just tired? Whatever the reason, as Dominic raised his hands to take hold of the puppy, she somehow found herself swaying helplessly towards him.

'Kate...' he breathed unsteadily as his arms closed about her.

'Hey, be careful!' she gasped breathlessly. 'You're squeezing the puppy to death!'

'To hell with the damn puppy!' he growled, staring intently down into her blue eyes. 'It's *you* I'm interested in—as you well know!'

His arms tightened convulsively about her. 'Kate!' he groaned as he buried his head in the fragrant cloud of her wild tawny hair. And then his lips moved slowly down over her brow, across her flushed cheek before his mouth took possession of hers. His kiss was a revelation. The mouth moving over her soft, trembling lips was a delight in its sensitivity and warmth. Never could she have believed that such a hard, stern man could be so gentle and tender, and, overcome by an avalanche of emotions she hadn't even known existed, she couldn't prevent herself from moving her body innocently and sensuously against him.

Dominic's tall frame shook in response to her erotic movements, his kiss deepening as he parted her lips and plundered the softness within.

It was as if she was drowning... Kate thought bemusedly. Drowning in ecstasy! And it wasn't until she became aware of the sound of soft, squeaky protests that she remembered the little dog clasped so tightly in her arms.

'No...! Please...the puppy...!' she gasped, tearing her lips away from his, as he slowly released the pressure of his arms. Gently taking the small creature from her, Dominic walked over to put it down in the cardboard box beside the stove.

Fearful that her trembling legs were going to collapse beneath her, Kate grabbed hold of the back of a nearby chair, clinging to it for dear life as he straightened up and turned to face her.

There was a long, long silence as they both stared at each other, broken at last as he cleared his throat and huskily informed her, 'This really won't do, Kate. I think it's about time that we...'

'I know...I know...' she muttered through nervously chattering teeth. 'I'm sorry. I don't know what came over me, I...'

'Precisely the same thing which came over me, I imagine,' he pointed out with a wry, sardonic twist to his lips as he walked slowly towards her. 'However, there seems to be little either of us can do about it,' he murmured, drawing her gently back into his arms once again.

'But...but you're still engaged to Helen, aren't you...?' she queried breathlessly, desperately trying to cling on to some sort of sanity, despite the fact that her body was still on fire from his lovemaking.

Dominic sighed as he lowered his dark head towards her. 'Yes, I suppose technically I am, but...'

'I—I'm sorry, but it's just no g-good,' she stammered, wrenching her shaking body from his arms. 'I know it must sound pretty dumb and stupid to you. But . . . but the truth is, Dominic, that I'm just a boring, old-fashioned type of girl . . .'

'I'm well aware of that.'

' . . . And unless and until you're definitely *not* engaged to Helen, I . . . I want you to stay well away from me!' she cried tearfully, before spinning on her heel and running from the kitchen as if the devil were at her heels.

'Come on, Kate, wake up! That's the third time I've had to ask you to pass the marmalade.'

'What . . . ? Oh, I'm sorry, Martin. I guess I was just daydreaming,' Kate murmured, handing him the small glass bowl. 'Any news from . . . er . . . Dominic?' she asked carelessly, eyeing the stack of post on the dining-room table in front of him.

'No, I don't think there's anything here from Hong Kong,' said Martin, quickly sorting through the pile and tossing letters down the table towards Alice and Aunt Laura. 'The last set of instructions he sent me were all concerned with estate matters. Since he's been away, old Dom has always seemed quite confident about our ability to stage the battle. So, if you're worrying about how the show is going to go today, I should relax.'

I only wish I could, Kate thought, staring gloomily down at her plate of fried egg and bacon. It was well over three weeks since Dominic had left the Priory in such a hurry—early on the Monday morning, following their last fraught encounter in the kitchen the night before. She hadn't even had a chance to say goodbye, and despite burying herself in all the arrangements for the Civil War battle, due to take place early this afternoon, there seemed to be a gigantic, aching hole in her heart.

All those romantic English poets seemed to have got it wrong, she told herself glumly. Because, while she obviously wasn't an expert, she was rapidly coming to the conclusion that falling in love was sheer, unadulterated hell. She had absolutely no idea of Dominic's true feelings. And, since she'd made it very plain that she wasn't prepared to get involved with him while he was still engaged to Helen, maybe he wouldn't want to have anything more to do with her anyway?

Even thinking about whether Dominic really cared for her seemed to be a pure waste of time, she thought helplessly. She was almost certain that Helen would never willingly let him go, and Dominic was undoubtedly the upright, honourable sort of man who might well feel that, once having made a promise, he'd have to honour it.

Feeling almost seasick as the arguments swayed back and forth in her brain, Kate was jolted out of her dismal reverie by a loud exclamation from Jayne Bailey, sitting down the other end of the table.

'Hey, Kate, you've managed to get *terrific* coverage in this morning's *East Anglia Daily News*! That interview you and Martin did for the local TV station seems to have really paid off. It's my guess that you'll have a record crowd of people here this afternoon.'

'Well, if we do, it will all be thanks to you,' Kate pointed out with a smile. 'In fact, what we'd have done without you, I've no idea.'

'Hear, hear!' echoed Martin, beaming at Kate's friend, who had responded to their urgent SOS a few days ago, and had proved to be such a tower of strength. 'As a publicity director, you've been brilliant.'

'Well, since handling the PR and publicity for my firm is what I do for a living, I can't say it's been too hard a task to work for you guys,' Jayne said modestly. 'However, we've got heaps to do, and I think we ought to check out those costumes, Kate, don't you?'

'You're right,' Kate agreed, getting up from the table and accompanying Jayne upstairs. All the arrangements for the battle had been going so splendidly that it had been a considerable shock to receive a telephone call, four days ago, from the Living History Society's manager. It appeared that at a mock battle which had taken place the previous weekend in Yorkshire both the Parliamentary and Royalist generals had suffered accidents; one breaking his leg, and the other being knocked out by a stray blow from a wooden pike.

'They're both recovering well, but I can't see either of them being fit enough in time for your battle,' the manager had told her. 'There's no need to panic, since the various regiments have their own officers and will be able to co-ordinate the show between them. However, you'll need to find two people to take their place. And...oh yes, they'll need to wear the right costumes, and be mounted on horseback, of course.'

It was that phone call which had prompted Kate to get in touch with her old friend Jayne. And the girls had soon decided that Martin and Osborne would fit the bill perfectly. Jayne had agreed to hire the costumes in London—from the shop where Kate had already ordered seventeenth-century dresses for herself, Aunt Laura and Alice—and bring them up with her to Norfolk.

Unfortunately, when she had told him about the new arrangements, Martin had looked at her with horror. 'You want *me* to get dressed up in satin and velvet? No way! I've already arranged to act as a gunner, helping to fire the cannons,' he'd added quickly, remaining deaf to all her pleas for him to solve what was clearly a major problem.

Osborne had also proved to be a man of straw. 'I'm sorry, Miss Kate, but there are some things a butler really cannot be expected to do—and wearing fancy dress is one of them,' he had said firmly.

'But what am I going to do?' she'd moaned to Jayne, when her Canadian friend had arrived at the Priory.

'Well, you were practically born on a horse—so why don't you take on the Cavalier role?' Jayne suggested. 'You're as tall as Martin, and I reckon the costume I've brought for him will fit you perfectly.'

'Gee, thanks, pal!' Kate had ground out bitterly. 'But what about the other role? Who can we find to take Osborne's place?'

'What about George Wakeham?' Alice had suggested with a grin. 'Why not get him to play the part of the Parliamentary general—"Roundhead" is a perfect description for George!' she had laughed. 'Besides, we all know how smitten he is by your charms!'

'Oh, very funny!' Kate had groaned, fed up to the back teeth with the jokes and teasing she'd had to put up with from her cousins. Goodness knows, she'd given no encouragement to the land agent, whom she'd met at the dinner party on the night of her arrival. However, 'Boring George' had apparently decided that he was madly in love with her—and had been haunting the Priory for the past three weeks.

Unfortunately, no one had come up with a better suggestion, and she'd been forced to ask him to take on the role.

'I'm not too keen on horses—and I don't think they like me, ha, ha!' he had laughed nervously, before adding with a leer, 'But you know I'll do *anything* for you, Kate!'

'Cool it, George,' she'd told him firmly. 'I just want you to sit in the saddle—and please try not to fall off.'

However, having seen him gingerly walking a horse around the stable yard, she had severe reservations about his ability to play the part.

And, later in the day, with only an hour to go before the show was due to start, she was still worrying about the problem.

'What are we going to do if George *does* fall off his horse?' she asked Jayne, who was helping her to get dressed.

'What can you do? He'll just have to climb back on again, won't he?' her friend replied callously.

'I can hear the drums!' Martin yelled with excitement as he burst into the bedroom, running across to hang out of the open window. 'Yes, I can just make out their flags, far away across the park!'

'OK, we're almost ready,' muttered Kate, tugging on her long, soft leather boots.

'People are still pouring into the park—it looks as if we're going to get a crowd of around at least five thousand people. But so far everything seems to be going very well,' he assured them before dashing out of the room.

'You look marvellous! Just like that painting of Gainsborough's, *The Blue Boy*,' Jayne enthused, gazing at Kate's tall, magnificent figure as she strode across the room towards a large mirror. Seeing Kate clothed in a tight-fitting sapphire-blue doublet with deep lace cuffs over matching knee-breeches, trimmed in lace and bows of blue and silver, Jayne was quite convinced that her friend was going to be the star of the show.

Kate grimaced at herself in the looking-glass. 'I'm not mad about myself in drag,' she murmured doubtfully, adjusting the high collar of fine white lawn and heavy lace which flowed down over her shoulders.

'Don't forget your hat.' Jayne picked up the sapphire blue, wide-brimmed felt hat trimmed with long, sweeping white ostrich feathers.

'Have I really *got* to wear this? I wish I was wearing a gorgeous, sexy dress like you,' Kate grumbled, enviously eyeing the other girl's low-cut deep emerald satin gown.

'Relax!' Jayne grinned. 'I know you might feel a bit odd, dressed up in a man's clothes. But there isn't really any alternative, is there?'

'No,' Kate sighed. 'Well, I suppose we'd better go and see if George wants some help getting into his costume,' she added as Alice burst into the room. 'Quite frankly, Jayne, I just *know* he's going to be a total disaster!'

'Don't worry about George,' Alice panted urgently. 'We've got a *real* disaster on our hands. Helen has just turned up. She's downstairs in the hall right now—screaming with rage and threatening to stop the show!'

CHAPTER EIGHT

'WHAT on earth is Helen doing here...?' gasped Kate, staring in consternation at Alice who, like the rest of the family, was dressed in seventeenth-century costume.

'I'm not entirely sure. She was creating such a row, and making so much noise, that it was all rather confusing.' The younger girl shrugged. 'As far as I could tell, Helen was absolutely furious about the TV and Press coverage. Apparently her father rang her up in London last night, and told her all about it. It seems the general thought she'd be pleased—instead of which, she's now going bananas!'

'Is that the girl who's going to marry your brother?' asked Jayne.

'Er...yes,' Kate interjected quickly. She'd told her old friend about the disastrous state of her relationship with Dominic, but she was anxious that Alice shouldn't suspect anything.

'Why should Dominic's fiancée be so upset about this mock battle?' Jayne queried with a puzzled frown.

'Because she didn't want it to be held here in the first place,' Alice told her. 'Helen has a thing about this house—she practically wants it to be kept in mothballs, if you ask me! And she was furious when Dom asked Kate to see to the arrangements.'

'Well, it's too late for her to do anything about it now,' Kate told them, rapidly recovering her equilibrium. 'As far as I'm concerned, she can yell as loudly as she likes, because no one will be able to hear her. Especially once the cannons start firing!' she added with a grin.

'I'm not sure you're right,' Alice told her with a worried frown. 'When I left the hall, Helen was claiming that she'd taken out a legal injunction which would stop the battle taking place, and demanding that Mother must take what she called "appropriate action".'

'Oh, lord, this is beginning to sound as if we've got a serious problem.' Kate grimaced. 'What did your mother say?'

'You know Mother!' Alice gave a nervous giggle. 'She was so frightened by all the noise Helen was making that she just went completely to pieces. Even *I* couldn't understand what she was saying.'

The three of them were still trying to think what to do when Martin came back into the room.

'Great news!' he called out happily. 'I've just had a call from Dominic. He got back from Hong Kong this morning, and phoned from the Rolls to say that if Mr Lewis puts his foot down on the accelerator he ought to be with us in about twenty minutes.'

However, his face fell, and he quickly became very worried and concerned when they told him about Helen's sudden arrival at the Priory.

'I'd say that just about puts the lid on the whole show,' he told them grimly. 'After all, Dominic's a lawyer, isn't he? And if Helen really *has* got a legal piece of paper saying the battle can't go ahead, then I don't see how he can ignore it.'

'We've put a lot of hard work and effort into getting this battle staged, and I'm not going to give up that easily,' Kate said stubbornly. 'It's beginning to sound as if we must somehow try and stop Helen showing Dominic that paper, right?'

'Oh, that reminds me—I nearly forgot to give you this note from Gorgeous George,' Alice told Kate, pulling a folded piece of paper from the pocket of her long gold satin dress.

Kate sighed with exasperation. 'Why should George be sending me a letter? Especially when the stupid man ought to be busy down the corridor changing into his costume.'

'Oh, no, he's not,' Alice was saying as Kate opened the note. 'The last I saw of him, he still had his ordinary clothes on, and was creeping off down the back staircase.'

'George Wakeham is the least of our worries at the moment...' Martin was saying, amazed to see his cousin, after quickly scanning the letter, run swiftly out of the room and down the corridor.

'I might have known it—*the skunk*!' Kate's voice was heavy with disgust as she looked around the room. There was the large wicker basket, empty now of the period costumes hired from a shop in London. And there, still laid out on the bed, were the clothes designed to be worn by the Parliamentary general.

'What's going on?' Martin asked in bewilderment as he and the others joined her in the bedroom.

'George has cut and run—the lily-livered rat!' Kate handed him the letter. 'He says he's thought it over, and he doesn't feel he can take part in the show. What a fink, huh?'

'He wasn't very keen on dressing up,' Alice pointed out. 'Especially when he discovered that you'd originally ordered the clothes for Osborne, who's so much taller than he is.'

Jayne slumped down into a nearby chair. 'Well, folks, I guess that's it. I don't see how you can beat a legal injunction *and* replace a missing general, all in the space of half an hour!'

'Oh, yes, we can!' Kate declared forcefully. 'I'm not giving up now. What about the thousands of people out there, who've paid their entrance money and are expecting an afternoon's entertainment? If there isn't a show, I can guarantee we'll have a riot on our hands!'

'But what are we going to do?'

As Alice's wail echoed around the room, Kate tried to cudgel her brains. Leaving aside the unexpected arrival of Dominic—and it was difficult to control her rising feelings of excitement at seeing him again—there was still the matter of how to deal with Helen, and to find a replacement for that ratfink George Wakeham. And then, gazing at the black velvet costume laid out on the bed, she suddenly realised that there might be a solution to their problems after all.

'Panic not, kids!' She gave a nervous gurgle of laughter. 'I think I've found the answer, but it's going to need a heck of a lot of luck, and some very careful planning.' She took a deep breath. 'OK, now here's what I want you all to do...'

Twenty minutes later, having seen the chauffeur-driven Rolls-Royce drawing up outside the Priory, Kate made her way across the now deserted hall and entered Dominic's study. The tall figure staring out of the window didn't hear her approach, and it was only when she gave a nervous cough that he spun around to face her.

'I'm glad I'm back in time for the battle, although whenever I see anyone, they seem to abruptly vanish again,' he said, his gaze narrowing at the sight of Kate's tall figure in her sapphire blue, slim-fitting costume. 'Even Martin only dashed in here for a moment, to say hello, and I haven't set eyes on him since.'

Kate nearly sagged with relief. Well done, Martin! And, since there was no sign of Horrid Helen, it looked as if Jayne and Alice had also successfully completed their mission. However, she mustn't get too confident—so much depended on the man standing in front of her. Staring at Dominic's tall, broad-shouldered body, clothed in a casual hacking jacket over an open-necked, cream-coloured shirt and tan trousers, she had to take a deep breath as she felt her heart turn over. For a moment, her resolution failed her. How could she ever hope to outwit this handsome man, with whom she was so much in love?

'Er...we do seem to have a bit of a problem, I'm afraid, and you're the only one who can sort it out,' she began nervously. 'But I think we'd better go upstairs. It's far too noisy to explain everything down here,' she added, raising her voice as the pipes and drums of the marching army began to sound loudly outside the window.

He looked at her with a puzzled frown for a moment, then shrugged his shoulders. 'You're probably right—we can't talk with all that racket going on. However, I'm feeling a bit jet-lagged, so I hope your problem is a fairly simple one.'

'Oh yes, it is,' she assured him earnestly.

'Hmm . . . well, before we get to this problem of yours, would you mind telling me why you're wearing a man's costume?' Dominic enquired, taking a firm grip of Kate's arm as they mounted the staircase. 'Not that I'm complaining, of course,' he added with a sardonic grin. 'You're definitely a sight for my jet-lagged eyes. Although I do feel you'd look far more attractive without that ridiculous hat.'

'It's not ridiculous,' she protested as he reached over, sweeping the hat from her head and allowing her long tawny hair to tumble down over her shoulders.

'That's better,' he murmured.

Kate wasn't at all sure that it was. So far, everything had seemed to be going according to plan. Almost too well, she thought, glancing cautiously up through her lashes at the man beside her, only to be thrown into a mass of nervous apprehension by the gleam in his clear blue eyes.

With dismay, she noted that Dominic didn't look at all jet-lagged. How on earth was she going to get through the next five minutes, when all she longed to do was to throw herself into his arms? And, with the certain knowledge that his keen, incisive brain would quickly cut her to ribbons if she didn't watch out, she could feel her heart sinking down into her soft leather boots.

'Well, here we are,' she said brightly, assuming a cheerfulness she certainly didn't feel, as she halted and opened a door.

'What are we doing here?' Dominic frowned as he glanced about the room, empty save for a large wicker basket, a few chairs and what looked like a suit of clothes laid out on the bed.

'I ... er ... I thought ... maybe we ought not to be alone together in my bedroom,' she explained, casting her eyes down in what she hoped he would assume was female modesty.

'Oh, really? Are you seriously suggesting that the mere sight of your virginal bed is guaranteed to provoke my rampant lust?' He raised a dark, sardonic eyebrow. 'If so, Kate, I must tell you you're quite wrong. I've got all the incentive I need standing right here in front of me!'

Kate's cheeks flushed as she quickly decided to drop the subject, and to press on with the urgent matter at hand.

'Er ... how did your trial go?' she asked.

'My what?'

'The law case ... in Hong Kong. Did you win it?'

'Oh, yes—yes, I did.' He gave an impatient shake of his head. 'However, that has nothing to do with ...'

'You must be tired after your long flight. So why don't you sit down?' she said, pointing to a comfortable armchair on the far side of the room.

As he shrugged, turning his back on her for a moment to walk over towards the chair, she quickly shut the door, turning the key silently in the lock.

Dominic gave a heavy sigh. 'All right, Kate,' he said sternly, easing himself back in the cushions. 'What's all this about?'

'Sure. Well, the thing is...' she began, proceeding to tell him what had been happening during the three weeks he'd been away, up to the arrival, yesterday, of the Living History Society members, who were to enact the battle between the Royalist and Parliamentary armies.

'Now you don't have to worry, because everything is under control,' she assured him. 'Both Martin and Osborne have been terrifically efficient, and my friend Jayne has done wonders over the publicity. The members of the Society are camping in the field beside the stables, and there's been absolutely no damage to either the house or the surrounding buildings. OK?'

'It sounds as though everything has been going very smoothly in my absence. However, I completely fail to see why you're wearing that male costume. I did see Alice, just now. It was, admittedly, a very brief encounter,' Dominic added wryly, surprised to note the sudden guilty look on Kate's face. 'Strange as it may seem, I'm not used to my sister taking one horrified look at me before shrieking with terror and quickly disappearing from sight!'

Kate shrugged, trying to look as if she too was mystified by Alice's nervous reaction to her brother's presence. 'The reason all the family are dressed in costume—other than Osborne, who refused to wear fancy dress—is that they're all playing the parts of their ancestors,' she explained, quickly changing the subject. 'Aunt Laura is Lady Farrell, who was alone here with her children and the household during the Civil War, while Jayne and Alice are acting the parts of her two daughters.

'There isn't actually anything for them to do,' Kate continued quickly. 'Other than stand around outside the house looking decorative, of course. But the Society's manager said it would sort of lend colour to the production.'

'Oh yes, I'm sure it will,' Dominic agreed drily. He brushed a tired hand through his hair. 'Now, I'm still waiting to hear about your problem.'

Kate hesitated for a moment, and then, taking a deep breath, she began to explain why she was dressed as the Royalist general, and her problem with George Wakeham's disappearance.

'We haven't got much time before I, and the person playing the part of the Parliamentary general, have to be on public display in front of the crowd,' she told him.

'To do—what?' he echoed.

'Well, apparently we have to meet up and pretend to have something called a parley. That's when I refuse to surrender the house to your army; and you have to say, "Bad luck, buddy, because that's going to mean a knock-out, drag-out fight".'

'A battle for possession of the Priory, in fact?'

She nodded. 'That's it.'

'All right. I get the idea—and I can even appreciate your problem.' He paused, regarding her intently for a moment. 'However, I spend a lot of my time in court, listening to witnesses giving evidence,' he continued smoothly. 'And I don't particularly care for the way this general of the Parliamentary army—obviously an evil fellow!—

has suddenly become identified with myself. The use of the word "you" was, I hope, a mere slip of the tongue?' he drawled.

'You're so sharp you'll cut yourself one of these days!' Kate said with a sigh of bitter exasperation. 'All right, I *was* hoping to lead up to it gradually. But the fact is, you're going to have to take over the part from George Wakeham.'

Dominic gave a snort of harsh laughter. 'Oh, no, I'm not!'

'Well, I'm afraid you *are*,' she retorted. 'I've locked this door and hidden the key about my person. So—if you don't get into those clothes over there on the bed, there's going to be no show, no battle—and a full-scale riot, with about five thousand people running amok and demanding their money back!'

'I'm damned if I'm going to let you blackmail me like this!' he stormed, quickly rising to his feet and striding across the room towards her.

'Hey, calm down!' she muttered nervously as he gripped her shoulders and gave her an angry shake. 'You'd be perfect in the part. I know you're a brilliant rider, and you look really great on a horse.'

'Flattery will get you nowhere! It won't take me five seconds to get hold of that key you've got hidden about "your person",' Dominic ground out through clenched teeth.

'I'll sue you for assault if you do!' gasped Kate, desperately trying to wriggle away from the fingers biting into her soft flesh. '*And* I'll have thousands of witnesses to back me up,' she added, twisting free at last, and running over to the open window.

'Why don't you come and take a good look at the problem?' she called out over her shoulder.

Swearing violently under his breath, Dominic joined her.

Leaning out over the stone windowsill, he gazed down on the huge crowd below, who were clearly enjoying a day out in the sunshine. Eating their picnic lunches or buying hamburgers, hot dogs and ice creams from the various stalls dotted about the park, they were gradually making their way towards the wide, grassy mound from which they would watch the spectacle; a ripple of excitement and noise stirring their ranks as the Roundhead army marched into view.

'I can't believe this is happening to me!' he hissed savagely.

'Ah, come on, Dominic. It's no big deal,' Kate pleaded, turning her head to face the hard, stormy eyes only inches away from her own.

'That's what you think!'

'If you'd just take a look at it, you'd see that the costume for the Roundhead general is as dark and plain as can be. In fact, you won't look very different from how you were dressed the very first time we met, will you? I mean, if you can put on all those weird clothes for the Lord Chancellor of England, you can do it for your family, right? Besides,' she grinned suddenly, 'I think you look really *terrific* in black velvet!'

Dominic gave a bark of angry laughter. 'Why, of all the girls in the world, did I have to fall in love with the most irritating, obstinate, aggravating and provoking female I've ever had the misfortune to meet?' he grated, pulling her roughly into his arms.

'*Dominic!* Do you really mean you...? Oh, lord, we're running out of time,' she gasped as the noise outside grew even louder. 'All those people out there...'

'They can wait!' he growled thickly, staring down at her soft, trembling lips for a moment, before his silvery-black head came down slowly towards her.

It felt as though it was years since she had been held in his arms, but from the very first moment his mouth took possession of hers, all sense of time and motion was wiped clear from her mind. As she leaned weakly against his strong body, her hands moved up to clasp themselves around his neck, her fingers burying themselves in his hair as her mouth opened beneath his, responding passionately to his kiss.

A storm of desire flooded through her mind and body. Oblivious to the noise and commotion out in the park, she was aware only of his strong hands holding her firmly against him; the deep thud of his heart beating in unison with her own, and the aroused force of his body clearly evident in their deep, intimate embrace.

When he finally released her, Kate could only gaze helplessly up at him as he slowly raised his hand, gently tracing the outline of her mouth with a finger that shook with tension.

Dominic sighed heavily. 'I know I'm going to regret this, but I can't see that I've any choice in the matter. So yes, I'll play the part of this damn general,' he said huskily. 'Now, for goodness' sake get out of here before I change my mind!'

Standing breathless outside the door, Kate leaned up against the wall, still shattered by the storm of passion Dominic had aroused in her, and trying to convince herself that she'd heard him correctly. He had *really* said he loved her . . . hadn't he? But what about Helen? She certainly seemed to think she was still engaged to Dominic.

The questions ran hither and thither like mice in her brain, remaining unanswered as he opened the door and strode out into the corridor.

'Hey, you look great!' she exclaimed, gazing at his tall, handsome figure dressed in a black velvet costume, trimmed with scarlet ribbons amidst the snowy-white silk and lace falling from his throat and sleeves. In fact, she thought, her legs feeling quite weak for a moment, in that outfit he didn't just look great—he looked sensational!

'I'm crazy about your hat,' she added, grinning up at the wide-brimmed black hat, decorated with a silver buckle and long scarlet ostrich feathers, which he was wearing at a rakish angle on his head.

'Watch it, Kate! I'm only going through with this nonsense in order to escape a lynching from that crowd out there. But I could very easily change my mind—so don't push your luck!' he warned her grimly, pausing for a moment to adjust the wide, sword-bearing sash worn across his body from shoulder to hip.

'For heaven's sake be careful with that sword.' She gazed anxiously at the heavy steel weapon. 'I tried lugging one of those around, but I decided to stick to a small ornamental dagger instead.'

'Very sensible. Have you got the horses ready?' he demanded, pulling on lace-trimmed, soft leather gauntlets over his long slim fingers.

'Yes, they're in the courtyard,' she muttered, gathering up her own hat and gloves, and having a struggle to keep up with him as he ran down the stairs.

There, as she had promised, a groom was holding their horses in front of the massed ranks of the Royalist army, which was remaining hidden from the crowd until the Roundheads had arrived. As they both sprang into their saddles, Dominic only had a moment to shout, 'I'll see you in front of the house,' giving her a brief wave of his whip, before riding off to join the Parliamentary army.

The beat of the drums increased, becoming loud and urgent as the two armies manoeuvred into position.

'Where's Kate?' demanded Jayne, almost jumping up and down with excitement on the stone steps leading down to the wide lawn in front of the house.

'Don't worry, she'll be here in a minute,' Alice told her, still feeling overwhelmed with relief at having escaped Dominic's wrath. Only for the time being, of course, she reminded herself, gazing across to the massed ranks of the Roundhead forces, where her brother seemed to be in deep conversation with a stocky man wearing ordinary clothes.

'What's George Wakeham doing over there?' Aunt Laura asked, raising her hand to shield her eyes from the glare of the afternoon sun. 'I thought you said he'd disappeared?'

'Umm... I thought he had,' Alice said faintly, watching open-mouthed with astonishment as her brother raised his whip in a threatening gesture. A moment later they, and the huge crowd, burst into gales of laughter as George took to his heels, closely followed by Dominic on horseback as he began chasing the plump, tubby figure from the arena.

It was an unequal match. George, zigzagging wildly across the lawn as he strove to evade the black horse at his heels, made the mistake of looking fearfully back over his shoulder once too often.

'Oh, help, I think I've got a stitch!' gasped Alice, convulsed with mirth as she watched George being helped from the arena, after having run full tilt into a massive cannon at the side of the lawn. 'Serve him right for leaving us in the lurch!'

'Yes, it does,' Jayne nodded, wiping the tears from her eyes. 'But I wonder why your brother was looking so angry...?' she began as the loud-speaker crackled into life.

'And now, ladies and gentlemen, you can see that both sides in this battle have mustered their troops, regiment by regiment,' the commentator's voice boomed out over the tannoy as Kate, followed by some of her cavalry officers, rode slowly out into the arena. 'The guns are now in position, and the Roundhead general is riding forward to parley with the Royalist defender of Thornton Priory.'

'I don't really know what I'm supposed to say to you,' Kate grinned as Dominic rode up, the smile drying on her lips as she noted the grim, tense expression on his face.

'Don't worry—I've got plenty to say to *you*!'

She frowned. 'What on earth do you mean?'

'I mean I've heard all about the little romance you've been conducting while I was away,' he grated angrily.

'Are you kidding? What romance?'

'Did you think I wouldn't find out about the apparently hot, passionate affair you've been having with the local land agent?' Dominic gave a harsh laugh.

'Who...?' She looked at him in astonishment. 'You don't mean George Wakeham...? Oh, come on! You can't seriously believe I would...'

'Why not? Especially since, according to George himself, it's been a remarkably torrid relationship.'

'You must be nuts!' Kate shouted angrily. 'I wouldn't even give that rat the time of day! And if you're prepared to listen to his nonsense, you must be just about as stupid as he is!'

'Look here,' a Roundhead soldier, mounted behind Dominic, interjected quickly. 'If you two don't mind, we'd like to get on with the show!'

'Who's supposed to win this stupid battle?' Dominic demanded, his face taut with anger.

'We are, of course!' snapped Kate. 'You and your army are going to be driven from the field. With your tails well and truly between your legs!' she added spitefully.

'Oh, really? Well, we're just going to have to change that cosy little arrangement,' he snarled.

She gave a shrill, high-pitched laugh. 'Oh, yeah—you and who else? I mean, just look at that army you've got—it's pathetic! They couldn't fight their way out of a paper bag.'

'Even if you paid me, I wouldn't have that bunch of pansies on my side.' Dominic gestured towards the brightly dressed Royalist cavalry mounted behind Kate. 'First whiff of gunshot, and they'll be running home to Mummy!'

''Ere, just a minute! Who are you calling a pansy?' a large cavalryman demanded belligerently.

'Hey, calm down—take it easy,' a technician laying the loudspeaker cables interrupted quickly. 'It's only a mock battle, you know.'

'Mock battle or no mock battle, I refuse to be beaten by this . . . this male impersonator!' stormed Dominic, his temper by now completely out of control.

'You pompous male chauvinist pig!' Kate yelled, reaching forward in the saddle to slap him across the face with her glove.

'Ah, yes. The two generals do seem to have decided to fight for possession of the Priory.' The commentator gave a nervous laugh. 'We don't, of course, know who is going to win the battle, ladies and gentlemen—and at this stage, I wouldn't like to hazard a guess on the outcome!'

'You'll be sorry you did that,' Dominic hissed as Kate stared back at him, suddenly sobering up and realising that she hadn't just slapped the man she loved—but she'd also done it in front of thousands of people.

Feeling quite sick at the sight of Dominic's cheeks, pallid beneath the tan, his eyes glinting with fury and venom, she quickly wheeled her horse around to face her troops.

'OK, you guys, let's get this show on the road,' she told them defiantly. 'I don't know about you, but *I* intend to smash the living daylights out of these Roundheads!'

'Anyone who calls me a pansy, is going to live to regret it!' the huge cavalryman agreed, as they galloped back to join their main force. 'And if you've got a battle plan that's half as good as the way you ride, girl, I reckon we're in with a chance!'

Unfortunately, Kate soon realised that warfare in the 1640s wasn't quite as easy as it might seem. Quite apart from the intricate movements of the men and their cumbersome weapons, everything appeared to be happening so slowly. It seemed to take an age to manoeuvre the musketeers into formation, and an even longer time for the men to load and prime their guns, between each volley of blank shot.

'We'll be here till Christmas!' she moaned, before sending off a small cavalry force to capture some soldiers which Dominic had left unprotected.

As the afternoon wore on, the smoke from the large cannon filled the arena, making it very difficult to see what was going on. Wearing thick satin and velvet was proving to be a trial beneath the hot sun; and alas, it was gradually becoming clear to her that Dominic was no slouch—especially when it came to drawing up his own battle plan.

'Hey, that's cheating!' she shouted, spurring her horse out of danger as she only just evaded capture by a group of his men pretending to be first-aid orderlies.

How could Dominic be doing this to her? Kissing her passionately one moment, and then accusing her of goodness knows what nonsense the next. Surely he didn't *really* believe that she'd been playing around—and with Boring George, of all people!

And what about him and Helen? I hope Martin has got that awful girl locked up in a nice dark cellar, Kate thought viciously, remembering the plan she and her cousins had made earlier this afternoon. Of course it had been vitally important to keep Helen out of everyone's way for as long as possible. But, if Dominic wanted to stay engaged to his rotten fiancée, that was certainly all right by her! But he was going to have to learn that he couldn't go around making mad, passionate love to other girls. What a double-crossing rat the man was! Oh, boy, she'd teach him a lesson he wouldn't forget in a hurry!

'I reckon we're in trouble,' a captain panted beside her as the Roundhead pikemen continued to advance slowly towards them.

'I'm *not* giving up!' she retorted. 'How do you know when these sort of battles are won, anyway?'

'Oh, you've got to capture their standard—that flag over there,' he explained, pointing towards a yellow and black pennant fluttering in the slight breeze.

'Right—I've had it! I'm going to get this battle sorted out once and for all,' she declared, digging her heels into her horse and galloping full tilt towards the far end of the arena. Not slackening her pace, she sped past the small groups of soldiers engaged in hand-to-hand fighting; past the knots of pikemen, with their weapons pointing outward like the spines of a porcupine, and jumping over a siege gun belching forth white smoke.

'Go for it, Kate!' Martin called out, his face covered with grime as he rammed another blank charge into the gun.

But she didn't hear him. Nor did she hear the buzz of increasing noise, as the watching crowd became aware—well before the Roundhead army—of her aim to seize victory from the ashes of defeat.

With her total concentration focused on the distant flag, she was oblivious to both the shouts and screams of the audience, and the commentator's hoarse excitement.

'Can it be done? Will the Royalist general capture the Parliamentary flag? It's going to be touch and go, folks! Oh-oh—now the Roundheads have realised the danger. Their general is galloping to the rescue. But will he be in time?'

Riding straight towards the small knot of soldiers around the flag, who quickly scattered in the face of her determined charge, Kate leaned sideways and seized hold of the wooden pole. Securely stuck into the ground, it refused to budge for a moment, and she was nearly unhorsed before it suddenly came away.

It was a sweet moment of victory, which Kate savoured to the full as she waved the flag above her head. However, she suddenly realised that she might have been celebrating too soon. Because pounding swiftly across the grass towards her was the unmistakable black figure of Dominic.

Since he was blocking the route back to her own side, Kate quickly spun her horse round. She could see that her only chance of escape was to make for a group of trees on the far side of the lawn, beside a paddock normally used for the horses. If she could get there before being captured, she might be able to weave her way among the trees, halting Dominic's progress, and giving herself the opportunity to double back and rejoin her army.

Her arms aching as she tried to balance the unwieldy flagpole, she urged her horse onward, her ears filled with the approaching thud of hoofbeats, echoing the thunderous pounding of her own heart. And then she suddenly felt her reins being seized. A second later she was brought to a halt with such force that she lost her stirrups and was swiftly catapulted out of the saddle.

Completely dazed and winded, she could only stare up at the sky, her eyes blinded by the shimmering rays of the late afternoon sun. Gasping for breath, it was some moments before she realised that she wasn't lying on the hard ground. By some miracle, it seemed that she had landed on a small stack of hay, just over the fence inside the paddock. And the reason why she couldn't move her limbs was not that she had injured herself, but because a heavy, familiar figure was lying on top of her.

'Hey, what do you think you're doing?' she croaked hoarsely. And when there was no reply or movement, she suddenly became frightened.

'Oh, Dominic!' she cried, frantically trying to lift her hands to his face. 'Oh, I'll never forgive myself if anything's happened to you,' she moaned helplessly. 'I really didn't mean any of those things I said—not one!'

'I'm glad to hear it,' he muttered, slowly raising his head and gazing down at her with wry amusement.

'I take it all back,' she said crossly. 'It was only because I thought something had happened to you—that you might have been hurt . . .'

'I am hurt. I seem to have banged my head on something,' he told her, wincing as he raised a hand to investigate a graze at his temple. 'It must have been that damn standard. When I wrenched it away from you, it got stuck in the ground, and I found myself being pole-vaulted down here.'

'Hmm, you look all right to me,' she retorted curtly. This two-faced rat needn't think he was going to get round her again—no way! 'We've got to get back to the battle. So will you kindly remove yourself, and let me sit up,' she added waspishly.

'No, I don't think so. I'm extremely comfortable where I am. Quite frankly, Kate, I really couldn't care less which side wins that battle. You and I have some talking to do,' Dominic said firmly. 'And this seems to be as good a place as any, don't you think?'

'We have nothing to talk about,' she retorted, trying in vain to wriggle out from beneath him, as he pressed his lips hungrily to her own.

It was always the same wonderful magic, she thought dazedly, her body trembling with desire as she responded to his kiss. It didn't matter how much they fought, or what insults they flung at one another. Ever since she had first met him, it had seemed that he only had to touch her, and she had melted helplessly in his arms.

Raising his head, he gently brushed the wild tendrils of hair from her brow, gazing down at her intently in silence for a moment, as if to implant her face in his memory for all time.

'You are totally incorrigible, and virtually unstoppable when you've set your mind to something,' he told her. 'Thanks to you, my family life appears to be in a complete shambles, and I also seem to have discarded a fiancée somewhere along the line.'

'Does that mean you aren't engaged to Helen any more?' she asked cautiously.

'You're quite correct—I'm not,' he agreed drily. 'I phoned her the morning I left for Hong Kong and told her it was all off between us.'

'But in that case, why did she come here today with a legal injunction to try and stop the show?'

'I've absolutely no idea.' He frowned and shrugged his broad shoulders.

Dominic may have given up Helen, but it sounds as if she hasn't given *him* up, Kate told herself, gazing up at him impassively as she strove to control the faint, trembling glimmer of hope flickering through her veins.

'And are *you* pleased that I'm no longer engaged to Helen?' he asked quietly.

'Me . . . ?' Her blue eyes widened in mock astonishment. 'What on earth has your broken engagement got to do with me?'

'Everything—as you well know!' he grated, a muscle beating frantically in his jaw.

'Oh, really. . . ?' she murmured.

For one awful moment she thought she might have gone too far—that he was going to explode with rage and fury. And then, with a strangled sound, pitched somewhere between a laugh and a groan, he buried his face in her hair.

'All right, you beautiful, impossible girl.' He lifted his head to give her a wry smile. 'I very much fear you'll drive me mad at least once a day—and twice on Sundays! But I find that I can't bear the thought of living without you, my darling Kate,' he said huskily. 'You've entered my bloodstream like a virus, and it seems there's no known cure. So—I can see no answer to the problem. I'm afraid you're going to have to marry me.'

'Is that the best you can do for a proposal?' she grumbled, trying not to grin. 'Whatever happened to the silver-tongued lawyer?'

'He's too much in love to think straight—let alone compose any flowery speeches,' he told her bluntly.

'Mmm, that's a lot better,' Kate breathed, her cheeks flushing as she gave him a wide, beaming smile. 'You're beginning to sound quite romantic!'

'I can promise to leave you in no doubt of my deep romantic feelings, my dearest one, just as soon as we're on our honeymoon in the South of France—I'm hoping to get married to you next Saturday, by the way. However,' he added urgently, 'since I can hear what sounds like an army of soldiers coming our way, I'd be grateful if you'd put me out of my misery as soon as possible.'

'Well, I kind of like the idea of the South of France. On the other hand...'

'Kate...!'

'Oh, Dominic, what an idiot you are!' She smiled tenderly up at him. 'I'm not at all impossible—I'm just madly in love with you, that's all. And no girl could be expected to be *entirely* sane in that condition, right? So of course I can't wait to marry you, and...'

But whatever else she might have said was lost as he gave a low husky laugh, before claiming her lips in a passionate, sensual kiss of deep possession and total commitment.

EPILOGUE

'AND how does the prisoner plead—guilty or not guilty?'

'Oh, guilty, of course!' Kate smiled radiantly up into the face of the lean, hard figure pinning her to the soft mattress. 'One hundred per cent guilty of loving you with all my heart,' she added tenderly.

'In that case, your sentence is imprisonment with me for life, I'm afraid.'

'That sounds just perfect!'

Dominic laughed. 'How about some more champagne?'

'Mmm, yes, please. I'm crazy about that vintage Krug. What a way to go!'

'You're not going anywhere—certainly not for the next week, anyway,' he told her firmly, rising from the bed and walking across the bedroom

'I guess I can hack it,' Kate laughed, leaning back against the pillows and gazing lovingly over at her new husband. How long had they been here in Nice, at the Negresco hotel? Four or five days? It sure was difficult to keep track of time—especially in this sumptuously decorated suite, with its amazing collection of Art Nouveau and antique furniture. In fact, other than a brief trip to the private beach opposite the hotel, and a few evening walks through the flowered terraces, they had hardly left their suite of rooms—or their bed!

Kate gave a happy sigh of deep contentment. Her husband was a wonderful, accomplished lover. And apart from one basic disagreement between them— he maintaining that the battle had been a draw, while she knew that *her* side had won, fair and square!—she was blissfully happy in her role as Dominic's wife.

Despite the rushed arrangements, it had been a lovely wedding in the old village church near the Priory, with Alice and Jayne as bridesmaids and Martin acting as Dominic's best man. The special licence had proved to be no problem—and a quick day's shopping in London with Jayne and Aunt Laura had taken care of all her bridal wear.

In fact, everything in the week following that crazy Civil War battle had conspired to make her wedding day a memorable one. A new school had been found for Alice—with a headmistress who had merely been amused when told of the girl's past tendency towards weird clothes. And even Martin, who had been gloomily facing the prospect of going to university, had been over the moon when his older brother had relented, allowing him to go to an agricultural college instead.

Delighted by her aunt and cousins' wholehearted approval of her marriage to Dominic, Kate had been worried to learn that Aunt Laura really was intending to leave the Priory.

'It's sweet of you to want me to stay here with you,' her aunt had said, her speech and conversation far more normal now that the threat of Helen had been removed. 'But to tell you the truth, dear, I must confess I've never been all that keen on this large house. Of course, it was different when Hector was alive,' she had added with a wistful smile. 'But now the children are growing up, I'm really looking forward to having my own small house—and to planning a new garden!'

'Do you really think she means it?' Kate had asked Dominic anxiously. 'I can't bear the thought of upsetting your family—and surely this house is big enough for us all to live in?'

However, he had confirmed that her aunt really did want the Dower House. 'You and I have already agreed that this is still Martin's home, even if he is going to be away most of the year at college. Alice will continue to spend her school holidays with us, of course, and as for upsetting my family, you have absolutely no need to worry. They all love you, my darling one, almost as much as I do!'

Reassured on that important point, it wasn't until two days before the wedding that Kate realised she had no one to escort her to the church. Wondering how she was going to solve the problem, she had been surprised when General Palmer had called at the Priory, especially to see her.

'Thought I'd come and wish you long life and happiness,' he had said gruffly, giving her a peck on the cheek. 'Now, my girl, your father was an old friend of mine. And since he's not here to give you away at your wedding, I wondered whether you'd accept my services?'

'What a terrific idea!' she had exclaimed, before realising that there was a major fly in the ointment. 'It's a bit awkward. I mean . . . Helen might not . . .'

'My daughter's gone off on a long holiday—with George Wakeham.' The General had shaken his head in disgust. 'Can't stand the fellow myself. But it looks as if they'll make a match of it. Just in case you're worried, I told Dominic when he got engaged to Helen that she wasn't the one for him. Just shows how right I was, doesn't it?' The elderly man had laughed good-naturedly.

'Well, in that case I'd be proud and happy to have you escort me to the church,' Kate had told him, smiling now as she remembered how kind and considerate the general had been.

'Do you think Helen really will marry that stupid man, George Wakeham?' she asked Dominic as he returned to the bed carrying a bottle of champagne.

Dominic shrugged as he poured her a glass. 'Who knows? Perhaps I should have been more angry with Martin for locking Helen in the dog kennels during the battle. But when George came to her rescue, and took her back home with him, I realised that the boy had done me a great favour after all.'

'She was as mad as a hornet!' Kate giggled, knowing she ought to be ashamed of being mainly responsible for Helen's temporary kidnap.

'Yes, it was very unkind,' he commented. 'Both you and Martin have a lot to answer for.'

'Well, what about you? Aunt Laura told me how you chased poor George right across the lawn in front of the crowd. That seems pretty unkind, if you ask me.'

'Believe me, he deserved it!'

'Well, I was thrilled to hear about you brandishing a whip in my defence,' she sighed happily. 'It all sounds terrifically romantic.'

'You are quite incorrigible,' Dominic said sternly, the effect of his words marred by the wide grin which matched her own. 'However, George is quite wealthy, and since he's clearly stupid enough to let Helen run his life for him, I expect they'll both be very happy.'

'All the same, Helen really is very beautiful,' Kate persisted, still feeling a stab of jealousy at the thought of his past relationship with the horrid woman.

'Now, my dearest one, I don't want to hear any more about my ex-fiancée,' he said firmly, removing her glass before clasping her tightly in his arms. 'I've noticed that you've been very careful not to raise the question,' he added. 'However, I can tell you that the answer is: no—I never went to bed with Helen.'

'You're kidding!' Kate looked up at him in amazement. 'She was so good-looking, I . . . well, I naturally assumed . . .'

'I'm telling you the truth,' he vowed. 'And if you're going to ask why not, I can only say that you were quite right. I did get engaged to her for all the wrong reasons—mostly to look after my home and family—and it undoubtedly served me right to discover, when it was far too late to withdraw from the engagement, that I didn't find her at all physically attractive.'

'Well, that's all right, then.' Kate sighed happily, leaning back against the pillows and beaming up at him. 'I know it shouldn't matter, but it did. I mean, I don't mind about all your other women . . .'

'Just a minute! What other women?'

'Hey, don't try and tell me you haven't had a whole bunch of girlfriends, buddy, because I know better! Nobody gets to be such a whizz at lovemaking—and you *have* to be the tops!—without a whole lot of practice.'

Dominic shook with laughter. 'My darling Kate, that is definitely the finest compliment anyone has ever paid me.' He lowered his head to give her a warm, tender kiss. 'Yes, of course I've had some girlfriends in the past. But that's where they are— in the past and long, long forgotten,' he added, an unmistakable note of deep sincerity in his voice.

'I bet they were all as slim as reeds,' she muttered, grimacing down at her own generous curves.

'Have you heard me complaining about your wonderful body?' he demanded sternly.

'No, well ... I can't say I have ...' She grinned, recalling their passionate lovemaking of just an hour ago.

'Surely you know that I'm crazy about very tall girls with voluptuous figures?'

'Oh, yes?' she laughed. 'I bet you didn't think that when we first met!'

Dominic shook his head solemnly. 'My dearest one, it's difficult to appreciate the manifold charms of a girl—however beautiful she might be—when she has just poured cement all over your precious car!'

'That was really awful of me, wasn't it?'

'I'm not going to argue with that statement,' he agreed wryly. 'However, on your first evening at the Priory, when you walked into the sitting-room wearing what I can only describe as the sexiest dress I'd ever seen ...' He paused and took a sip of his champagne. 'I can tell you, Kate, that it was like being struck by a thunderbolt. I was quite suddenly and totally in love!'

'Well, you disguised it pretty well—because you were simply horrid to me!'

'Ah, yes, I wasn't too kind,' he admitted with a sad shake of his head. 'But in my defence, I must tell you that when I look back, it seems as though I was walking barefoot through a field of broken glass! There I was, engaged to be married to another girl—which I'd already discovered to be a great mistake—and I had absolutely no idea how you felt about me.'

'I didn't realise it at first,' she admitted. 'But I reckon I must have fallen for you like a ton of bricks, practically straight away.'

'Well, you certainly managed to fool me!' Dominic told her gloomily. 'All I knew was that you'd burst into my well-ordered life with all the explosive force of unstable gelignite. You'd totally wrecked my beloved car, disrupted all my future plans, and appeared to be actively encouraging rebellion among my family.'

'Oh, come on! I wasn't *that* bad, surely?'

'Oh yes, you were!' He gave a short bark of laughter, smiling tenderly down at her with a consuming desire in his blue eyes, their coldness banished for ever. 'How I love you, you maddening, gorgeous girl,' he told her huskily. 'Even if we're married for over fifty years, I know I'll never be able to guess what's going to hit me from one minute to the next. And, strange as it may seem, I can't think of a happier fate!'

'You're just a glutton for punishment,' she teased, her pulse starting to race as his fingers began sensually caressing her soft skin.

'Oh, no, my dearest love,' Dominic breathed thickly, his touch becoming more pressing, more intimate. 'I'm a very lucky man—and I've got the good sense to know it!'

Take 4 bestselling love stories FREE

Plus get a FREE surprise gift!

• HARLEQUIN •
HISTORICAL

CHRISTMAS

• STORIES • 1992 •

Capture the magic and romance of Christmas in the 1800s
with HARLEQUIN HISTORICAL CHRISTMAS STORIES
1992—a collection of three stories by celebrated
historical authors. The perfect Christmas gift!

Don't miss these heartwarming stories, available in
November wherever Harlequin books are sold:

**MISS MONTRACHET REQUESTS by Maura Seger
CHRISTMAS BOUNTY by Erin Yorke
A PROMISE KEPT by Bronwyn Williams**

Plus, this Christmas you can also receive a FREE
keepsake Christmas ornament. Watch for details in all
November and December Harlequin books.

**DISCOVER THE ROMANCE AND MAGIC OF THE
HOLIDAY SEASON WITH HARLEQUIN HISTORICAL
CHRISTMAS STORIES!**